GW00480928

DEATH COMES TO TINSEL TOWN

Copyright November 2023 2nd Edition– Author: Debbie Nyman

Front cover illustrator: Elena Zinski of ZinskiArt

ISBN No. 978-0-9957289-8-1

Printed by:
Book Printing UK, Remus House, Coltsfoot Drive, Woodston, Peterborough, PE2 9BF

Dedication:

In memory of Mum, Dad, Nan and particularly Uncle Ron.

This book is also dedicated to my brother David, and sisters Anne & Gloria and all the family who will have to work out the fact from the fiction! With love, Queen Dx

<u>**Death Comes to Tinsel Town is the creation of Debbie Nyman.**</u>

Based on background factual stories that her Uncle wrote, she has turned this into a Murder Mystery using his facts and a rather large dose of fiction. The facts have been interwoven into a plot resulting in a murder.

Debbie, now partially retired, works part-time as a swimming teacher at a local school. Prior to this she worked as a Teleprompt operator in film and television. For over 25 years she was a volunteer at Great Ormond Street Hospital as a 16mm film projectionist.

Other books by the Author :
"Tea & Memories, Growing up in Roe Green Village." 2018. An historical account of the Village in Kingsbury from childhood memories of people who lived here through WW2. It has sold over 200 copies through word of mouth.

"A-M Wizz, The Absent-Minded Wizard". (Books, 1, 2 and 3), 2021. A children's book aimed at 6-9 year olds. 3 books, 7 stories in all. Stories showing being Absent-Minded can have positive outcomes with a bit of magic thrown in. Humorous and with amazing illustrations by ZinskiArt.

Facebook: www/facebook.com/DebbieNymanAuthor/

Purchase book: https://silvervixen.bigcartel.com/

PART ONE – FEMME FATALE

CHAPTER ONE

She entered my office like a Hollywood film noir femme fatale. All furcoat and no knickers came to mind. Her slender, shapely legs went further than my imagination allowed me. Smart, determined, with a demure walk and her chin held at a slightly haughty angle. It gave her an air of superiority which I found off-putting from the start.

"Detective Charlie Moray?" She didn't wait for my response.

"Diana Saunders." The loud tarty voice didn't match the elegant look she had strived to achieve. A certain amount of 'common' crept into her missing vowels.

"I've been recommended to contact you as I 'ear you are a no-nonsense PI and I am a no-nonsense mother of a wayward son," she curtly continued.

"Do take a seat Mrs Saunders," I waved to the well-worn leather chesterfield opposite my desk. She took a glance before taking a hand across the surface to make sure any dust would not touch the fur. She seemed satisfied. As she crossed her legs the fur coat opened to reveal that pair of legs I had imagined which led down to those enticing ankles. Did I mention how old she was? Well, for someone with those characteristics she must have really looked after herself and didn't look the 60 years she admitted to.

It seemed an age while I waited mesmerised for her to give me a bit more information than just a wayward son.

"Well, Mrs Saunders, or can I call you Di, I....," I didn't have time to finish my sentence before she put me in my place and spat back, "The name is Mrs Saunders; if you get to know me better, it's Diana to you."

I realised I was having to stay at arm's length if I wanted to keep this job but my gut instinct told me this was really a job for the law.

"Have you made any enquiries with the Police?" I suggested, as I had already half-decided this was not the job for me.

"Now, why would I go to the Police," she sneered. "What would they be able to do?"

"It sounds like a missing person, Mrs Saunders, and the Police would probably have better access to files and naturally, you wouldn't have to pay for that information." As I said it, I felt I was doing myself out of a job. Still, the alarm bells in my head told me I did not want this case, but Gumshoes, in those cheap detective novels I read, always ignored such advice.

She shook her head dismissively at me.

"You aren't listening Mr Moray, I want to find where he is first and then I intend to do a lot more with the information."

I still wasn't sure where she was coming from. I couldn't understand why she was so keen to find him; there had to be a motive behind her wanting a private detective.

"Are you available, or not?" she said in an accusing manner. "If you don't have the expertise, I'll go elsewhere," she interrupted my thoughts.

I was curious as to who had recommended her to me, as I imagine I was not her first choice and I wasn't exactly in the Top Ten of Detectives.

I decided to change tactics and put on my best former Policeman smile.

"Mrs Saunders, I'm sorry I gave you that impression," I said. "It's just that I wondered who had sent you to me, it's always nice to know if I have been recommended and by whom."

"It's nothing mysterious, Moray, in fact I'm surprised the name Saunders didn't ring a bell. My 'usband 'Arry got in a bit of bovver a few years ago and he said you got him off the 'ook, so to speak."

Harry Saunders? I vaguely recalled an elderly shabbily dressed man coming to my offices one rainy day but it was some years ago. He told me he ran the bookies in Kilburn and the Police were after him for betting out of hours. His place had been busted more times than a bank with the doors open.

In fact, I didn't put the Mrs and Harry as an obvious married couple. He never mentioned he was married for one thing and didn't look the type who would be buying anyone a fur coat. Mrs Saunders seemed out of his league so there was no reason to put two and two together and get Mr & Mrs.

Again she broke into my thoughts and uttered, "Are you available for hire?"

"Who for? Your husband?" I said momentarily confused.

"Listen, Mr Moray, I'm not here to work with a man who can't remember who I'm talking about from one sentence to another."

I hadn't worked for a number of months and like all hard-working ex police, I needed some food on my plate. I needed to concentrate.

"I'm sorry Mrs Saunders," I apologised, trying to sound interested without sounding too eager. "I was trying to remember your husband."

"Forget about that waste of space," she snapped, "he's dead anyway. I'm talking about his son, Wayne, a real chip off the old block who also turned out to be a waste of space like his father."

I asked her if she had anything to go on and if she had any clues as to where he might be now.

"He could be anywhere now," she said as she threw down a brown ragged edged book. "That's his address book. He was always in a hurry to leave and left that behind. You'll probably find all his 'girlfriends' in there and a few celebrities."

Diana made a gesture to open the book but then held back and said: "I'll add expenses to make a few phone calls to track him down."

Almost as an after-thought she produced another well-thumbed volume.

"Oh, and just for your amusement, here's a notebook, he left that too. I've read bits of it but he just goes on about how marvellous he has been and his time in the Navy. I've never bothered to read the whole lot, it started to make my stomach turn. I doubt if he's still in the UK. But anyways, be my guest and phone up a few of his friends, they won't speak to me so I didn't even try. I just want my money back and see him behind bars."

"What money?" my ears suddenly pricked up realising she had just given me the actual reason for trying to track him down.

"So he's not just a missing person then?"

"Of course not, my loving son," she said sarcastically, "managed to get away with thousands of my hard earned pounds. Do you think I'd waste my time looking him up? He stole from me. He's a no-good, gold digger of a son."

I was about to tell her my terms and conditions but she was equally ready to dictate *her* terms and conditions to me before I could breathe in.

She made it clear that the sky's the limit, so who was I to turn down my next 3-course meal?

"There's a lot of money at stake that I do not intend to kiss goodbye to," she said, "but that's for me to know and you to find out. All you need to know is that I'll make it worth your while."

I was quite intrigued to know what she thought would make it worth my while and let her continue.

"All expenses will be paid, and I mean *all*, but if I find you are wasting it on drinks and smokes and floozies, my contract with you will be cancelled."

She handed me a wad of money.

"That's the appetiser so you don't 'ang about and don't waste your time on any other jobs. Just concentrate your whole time on getting my money back."

All fine and dandy I thought but to do that I'd have to track Wayne down. At the time, I had no idea that this was going to take me from my offices in Cricklewood to the back streets of Kilburn and ultimately to the United States of America and the highlife in the hills off Sunset Boulevard and Hollywood.

"He worked with Marilyn Monroe, you know and that's just for starters. You name them, he worked with them. He worked at Paramount Studios before he disappeared."

She had thrown me a small nugget of a clue as to his whereabouts at some point in his life.

"Any son that is rotten to the core would not stoop to rob his mother. Wherever he is I shall get him, the world is small."

And with a flourish of her furcoat, she walked out of my office but into my life.

There were plenty of addresses but the strange thing about it was all the entries had been handwritten in pencil, like everyone was temporary, ready to be rubbed out and replaced.

I might add, aside from that one meeting with her, she made the occasional phone call if I hadn't been in touch for a while, and I would update her usually once a month. Somehow she knew that it might take some time to track Wayne down and then investigate what he had done with her money. If what she said was true, I had no idea what the reason was that she wanted to see him behind bars.

The strange thing about all this was that Wayne wasn't hiding from her, he just hadn't been in touch not even with his older brother, Lester; they were like strangers, estranged in their late teens even though they hadn't argued.

Diana Saunders was at the centre of the silence.

CHAPTER TWO

I sat in the office after Mrs Saunders left and started flicking through the pencilled addresses. There were some quite interesting names all right. Liberace, Yul Brynner, Debra Paget, Jane Russell, Mike Connors and yes, there she was in thick pencil, Marilyn Monroe. I didn't really believe Mrs Saunders but I was proved wrong by this entry in his address book. Very impressive. And amongst the celebrities were friends I assumed who I hoped would be accessible and generous enough to direct me to Wayne. I started to notice that there were strange symbols against names which I couldn't decipher but they must have meant something. I would have to look into that further.

I put the address book down and picked up the notebook.

Also handwritten but this time in pen, this small tattered book proved to be a spectacular insight into the family dynamics. The more I read, the more I was beginning to get something of a balanced view on the relationship between Wayne and his mother. There seemed to be a sibling rivalry with his older brother, Lester, competing for the attention of their parents; Wayne didn't feel he lived up to their expectations, whereas his brother, Lester, seemed to easily please his mother, and his father was always proud of what he did. It was Wayne's perspective on life and as I read on, he always seemed to be making plans to escape from the parental cage.

As the sun went down, I was still immersed in his notebook. There seemed a lot of desperation in the writings as he described his first escape to the Navy even though he was underage. There was a fair bit written in some sort of shorthand. I decided it was a good point at which to stop. Turning the lights off, closing the door and with the notebook and address book in my case, I walked towards my car and the short drive home.   It gave me time to reflect on my time as a policeman on the 'beat'. I loved the job but the late nights and bringing my work home, so to speak, was a strain on my marriage. Looking back, I can see why it failed, so much so that coming home unexpectedly one night it was no surprise to find my wife had packed up and left me. She had gone back to her mother's, who at first was so pleased that her daughter had married a cop but then started to drop huge hints on making her a grandmother. My shifts didn't help and we thought it would be less stressful. I could be my own boss and earn more money by starting up an agency.   It seemed to work for a while but there was something missing between us. Perhaps we had fallen out of love.

I put the car into gear and headed home – I was used to being alone now.

CHAPTER THREE – HARRY SAUNDERS

The next day I got to my office to find the post piling up on the floor unopened. It was just the usual bills and mail order rubbish, nothing that screamed out to be dealt with.

I was glad that would leave me a clear day and perhaps a chance to phone a few people in the address book. After all I had been paid enough up front to afford to take a day off and concentrate fully on Mrs Saunders versus son.

I flicked ahead in the notebook and found there was a real curiosity to meet the author. But first I needed to get more information about Mr & Mrs Saunders. What was her motivation to track down her son? The money was important but it seemed she had waited an awful long time to now go after him.

I went to my filing cabinet, still intact and in my archives I found my file on Harry Saunders. *Pity he was dead, I thought absently.*

He had come to me to get off a repeat warrant. He didn't want his wife to know, although hadn't mentioned her existence previously. It turned out that he had a close association with the Police, but for all the wrong reasons. The local law frequented his home for pay-offs, as well as social gatherings, but he still got arrested more times for betting out of hours in his own betting office. This time it was more serious and could have put him behind bars, the one place he wasn't keen to visit.

He was of Russian descent, the eldest of ten children and had made it the hard way. He had struck me as a man busy with his own affairs, so much so, that he hardly mentioned he was married or had children. I sort of guessed that he was married but I never asked and he never offered that information. My notes showed that the war had changed things for him. The dog tracks closed, and in closing took away one of his incentives for living, that's when he opened a gambling club in Kilburn, an unfashionable suburb of London, which was not far from his fashionable home where he entertained both the wealthy and notorious gambling set of London.

I had written a fair bit in my notes from the time when Harry visited me trying to get off a charge for the umpteenth time. I read through my notes again to see if there were any leads I could go on.

Horse and dog racing started up all over England in an effort to release the agonising tension of war and lack of entertainment. Harry Saunders' life immediately changed again. He had installed a tick-a-tape machine and partitioned off a small section of the Club. Here he mentioned for the first time, that he had two sons, Wayne and Lester. He got them in so that they could operate as a bookmaking team. He got Wayne to set up the "Book" as one of his daily tasks and change the tick-a-tape paper so it wouldn't run out at a crucial moment.

Turned out Lester was more mathematically inclined than Wayne.

Harry had taken me to his Club and showed me the section, known as, "The Pen". It had a high shelf with three telephones; two for incoming and one for outgoing calls. While the actual passing of money by hand was illegal, phone betting was not.

He got his sons to sit at the desk recording all the bets, while Harry stood beside them accepting the illegal money transaction bets, by answering the phones and shouting to the milling crowd. I could visualise the scene; studying the racing forms of the constantly new betting odds being delivered on the tick-a-tape machine; laying off bets to other bookies when he became overloaded on horses which, in his estimation, would put him too far in the red if they came in first, second or placed; and constantly shouting instructions to Wayne or Lester of new bets being made and bets he was laying off.

Harry said most times the "Book" would start at 11.00 a.m. and go on till 4.00 p.m. or even later, depending on the day's meetings. He lived well on the backs of people who couldn't even afford a "tuppeny" bus fare at the time.

But Harry hadn't come to me to chat about the way he ran his business, it was to give me the reason he needed to get off a charge.

It was the start of a normal, busy day at the Club. Everything was running normally until he looked over at Wayne and saw a tall stranger beside him. The stranger slowly put his right hand in the pocket of his light-coloured raincoat and withdrew it slowly to reveal a Police warrant card. Harry recalled that feeling once again as the stranger in the raincoat told him it was a raid and he put both of them under arrest.

Harry pleaded to let Wayne go as he was only a minor, which the Officer gave the nod and Wayne just stayed put.

The Officer then shouted instructions to his men who had quietly infiltrated the Club and gave out instructions.

Harry was arrested and marched out of the club by the police.

While the action was taking place, Harry had taken the opportunity to slip a large wad of notes from his trouser pocket for Wayne to slip under "The Book".

This was one of a few arrests but Harry was no fool and got away with a fair bit of illegal gambling. When he came to see me he didn't seem unduly worried about it but needed to stay out of jail.

He ended up paying a penalty and his club was closed down for a while.

I heard after some time, that poor Harry had a mental breakdown and in fact, passed away under rather suspicious circumstances. I felt this wouldn't be something I could enquire with Mrs Saunders but that Wayne might know what happened to his father.

It seemed that Mrs Saunders held the key, not only to her missing son but a whole lot more. It wasn't a key to a shed but to a Palace.

As time went on, the background to Wayne's disappearance, the missing money and more, was all about his mother.

CHAPTER FOUR

"Where the hell have you been until this time of night?"

"Just out to a movie."

"Till this time of night?"

"Yes."

"That all?"

"Yes."

"You bloody liar."

"But that's…" Wayne started to explain.

"You wait till the morning you dirty little stop-out. I'll give it to you. Now go straight to bed you dirty rotten stop-out."

*****

The phone rang, and Mrs Saunders stringent tones assaulted my ear.

"Have you found anything yet?"

I told her it was early days but I would need a photograph of Wayne and perhaps a little more information about when and where the money had changed hands.

"I'll look for a photograph if I haven't thrown them all away," she said reluctantly, then added, "have you read any of his notes yet?"

I decided to stall on that one and just said I had skimmed through sections but not sure whether it would throw any light on his whereabouts. In fact, his notebook was the key to his character; his reasons for leaving home and keeping his distance from his mother, but it wasn't going to help the situation by revealing these details.

Diana was happy to meet up and invited me to the house in Willesden: a detached, well looked after corner plot in a nice part of town. I wanted to see if she would offer a bit more information on Wayne plus the photograph and perhaps more about Harry too.

I stood in front of an imposing solid wood door and rang the bell and a young lady, who answered the door was their Irish maid, Geraldine. As it turned out Wayne had a lot to say about Geraldine and she in turn offered some insight at a later stage in my investigation.

"Charlie Moray, to see Mrs Saunders," I said.

Geraldine acknowledged this and said I was expected and to come in.

I entered the palatial front lounge to find Mrs Saunders comfortably seated, legs crossed and ankles showing beneath a silk dress.

"Do make yourself comfortable," she said softly and gestured towards a leather armchair which I could have happily slept in for a few days.

"Geraldine!" she shouted, "Bring us some tea, woncha," the delicate tone suddenly grating.

From the other side of the door, I could hear Geraldine shuffling into another room and within a few minutes, brought in tea on a trolley. It was the works; sandwiches without the crusts, little tea cakes and tea being poured into bone china cups.

Mrs Saunders had certainly done OK without Harry, or because of Harry.

"So you want to talk about my 'Arry? He always used to say: *All the men should live together and all the women should hang together.* I told him it should be the other way round and all the men should hang!" She gave out a laugh and I managed an awkward smile. "You know he went a bit mental after the war. I even had to section him for a while, he went right 'orf his 'ead. I ended up bringing up my boys single-handed most of the time."

"Do you have any photographs I asked?" She got up and went to her handbag and produced a much handled photograph of a handsome young man in Navy uniform.

She handed the photograph to me.

"That's Wayne, when he was a nice kid and not a thieving little bastard."

"Do you have any others and perhaps one of Lester as well?" I asked in the hope that she may have kept albums.

She had plenty of photograph albums for me to pick a selection of her boys. I took about 6 good photographs of happy family snaps.

"Is it OK if I take these ones, Mrs Saunders?"

"Oh, call me Diana as you're in my 'ome now," she said sweetly.

I placed the photographs in my wallet for later examination.

We passed some pleasantries and steered the conversation towards finding out a little of Mrs Saunders own background. She was turning out to be a woman of substance and some mystery. But her relationship with her husband was something I needed to investigate a bit further.

Geraldine came back in and started to clear the cups and tea away. It seemed an indication that it was time to go and a good moment to call this meeting to an end and make a new date.

As I left, I hesitated and decided to hang about a little longer to see if I could catch Geraldine as she left. She had worked for the family for some time and I presumed knew Wayne well. I had a feeling she might have some stories to tell and I wasn't wrong.

I saw her emerge from the front door and approached her as she walked briskly up the road. Geraldine initially walked even faster ahead of me so I called out to her.

"Geraldine!"

She stopped and turned towards me.

"I'm sorry Geraldine, but is there anything you know about Wayne that might help me find him?" I ventured.

"What if I don't want you to find him?" her response was surprisingly hostile.

It wasn't what I expected.

Slowly the story unfolded. It turned out that Geraldine had a real soft spot for Wayne. She had worked for the Saunders since Wayne was a youngster and had been his shoulder to cry on, which was on a regular basis. Yes, she had kept in touch with him. In fact, Wayne would write to her when he was in Port somewhere and get her up to date.

"Do you still have his letters?" I asked.

"Oh yes, of course," she replied with real emotion.

I knew it was quite an imposition but asked her if she was willing to share any of his words with me.

She was adamant that was not an option, these were all she had of Wayne and was reluctant to share them. But she was ready to speak about him. She knew he was still alive but strangely was not willing to give me his address.

"I don't want her to find him," she said. "She's done enough damage over the years."

"What do you mean by that?" I asked sympathetically.

"I don't like to say too much, I need this job," she replied desperately.

"I'm sorry, Geraldine, I really don't want anyone harmed but I have been asked to investigate and find Wayne."

She wasn't having it and felt she had already said too much.

"I don't want her to know that I hear from Wayne," she continued.

"Besides Wayne never put an address on his letters because he knew that his mother just might find a letter and didn't want her to have any idea where he was living. He also didn't want me placed in an awkward position and told me not to even mention that I received letters from him." It was solely a relationship between Wayne and Geraldine.

So really, all I found out was that Wayne was still alive.

One thing was for certain, I needed to meet up with Geraldine again.

CHAPTER FIVE

I realised I was going to have to get onto my old police pals to check out if they had a record on Harry Saunders and whether his wife might be known to the local constabulary.

It was a real eye-opener.

Harry had more "form" than the best race horse in Newmarket and Diana wasn't that far behind him. They were quite a couple.

Both of them had "previous" in the neighbourhood and were bound over in one case for twelve months for threatening behaviour and assault. I wondered how much of this Geraldine knew, as the couple must have gone missing sometimes and Geraldine did seem quite fearful of them, even too scared to leave. I wanted to try and meet with Geraldine again as she seemed to be the key to some of Wayne's life at home and saw him right up until he left for the Navy.

She was also there on the few times he returned.

It would have to wait as the following week Mrs Saunders called to make a date to meet me but this time at my office.

Diana didn't want Geraldine overhearing our conversation.

I wanted to follow up my tea conversation with Diana when she indicated that Harry had some kind of breakdown.   I needed to find out exactly what their relationship was all about. My enquiries at the local cop shop proved not only that Diana was capable of assault on others, but she had also been cautioned for beating up poor Harry.   No wonder he had a breakdown.

And of course, Wayne may well have been witness to all these events.

I opened our meeting by mentioning the address book and whether she knew what all the strange symbols might be. She said she had no idea. I referred to the notebook and that there was a fair bit in some sort of shorthand.

"No idea and not interested," she retorted back. "He was full of secrets and perhaps you can get the shorthand deciphered. I couldn't make head nor tail out of it."

I didn't divulge the information I had received from the police about their activities in the neighbourhood but I wanted to find out a bit more about her relationship with her husband. There had been a notebook entry where Wayne had just written *Dad breakdown*. Could she tell me any more about this?

"I don't really want to talk about it," Diana hesitated but then continued. "It was an awful time in our marriage. That said, I suspect if and when you catch up with Wayne, he'll tell you a different story. So it's best I tell you the truth, rather than what you'll hear from that useless cheat."

With that she began to explain that *the old boy* had been in hospital under observation for three days as he had been acting strangely. Harry kept insisting he was alright and wanting to go home but she was out to get him sectioned.

"I didn't want the old boy home, so went to the Medical Magistrate to try and get him certified but unfortunately for me, he was certified sane!"

She said they had agreed he wasn't well and needed medical attention and were willing to send him to hospital.

"I wasn't well too and couldn't face taking him on at home. The thought of him coming home made my heart sink," she said.

Apparently the Ward Sister wasn't too complementary about *the old boy*, saying he was a hopeless case and kept insisting on going home. Diana was in full flow now and called him all sorts of names, saying what an obstinate so-and-so he was but with the help of the Ward

Sister, she got Harry to sign a form sending him to Shenley Hospital.

Diana 'sold' the idea to him telling him it was a beautiful place, the grounds just magnificent. She added the information that it belonged to Raphael Tuck who had lent it to the government during the war for wounded soldiers. I wasn't sure whether that would have made Harry feel any better.

"I went home and felt that, thank God I was rid of *the old boy* for a couple of weeks in a place for those that are a bit screwy." She made a circular motion with her finger at her temple to demonstrate this fact.

"However," she said, "it didn't last. He was sent to hospital for an appointment and because he was a voluntary patient at Shenley, he insisted on coming home. I decided to ignore the whole business and didn't call the hospital until the evening. God was on my side as by the time I phoned, the hospital had kept him in. I remember," she added, "that there were a couple of Yiddisher men in the ward; one on his left and one on his right. The one on the left had taken 62 pills, as a rule 10 is sufficient to kill anybody but he was still alive. The other fella not only looked 'touched' but he didn't stop talking and when he had visitors who brought him food, he didn't stop eating either!"

Diana smiled, which was unusual for her.

"Just as I was leaving, he offered me some cheesecake the nutcase!" she exclaimed.

She remembered going home and thinking Harry certainly looked as though he had aged. But more important was that she didn't have to see his miserable face and hear his voice; the house felt peaceful and jolly without him and as a result, she began to have a good time and go out where and when she wanted to.

"You can close your file on him now, Moray, 'cos he's dead and not coming back to gamble away my money or even haunt me," she warned. "He had a heart attack in the end, you know, nothing to write home about."

I was holding the address book and wanted to know whether she had spoken to any of his contacts. She said she didn't really know his friends, just one, Guy Robertson living down in Cornwall. I made a note to call him at a later date. It was a strange admission on her part, as it turned out she was very well known amongst his friends but for all the wrong reasons.

Then out of the blue, interrupting my thoughts, she said: "I ran a restaurant with Wayne down Willesden High Road. We bought this place and I helped him run it, but like everything else it didn't last. He messed up and like his father, walked away from any real commitment."

Diana sounded bitter. "If you find him, he'll say he had a mild breakdown." She took a breath and continued, "the two of them would say that to avoid their responsibilities – I told you, like father, like son. He wasn't like his brother, Lester. Lester knew how to respect his mother."

This made me want to meet up with Lester. He seemed to have a different relationship with his mother and I wanted to know if he was in touch with Wayne. This was a meeting on the backburner for now though.

As if reading my thoughts, she said:

"All Lester knows is that Wayne cheated me out of a lot of money after all the support I gave his brother." Diana got to her feet.

"I need to leave now", she said rather abruptly. "I'll call you next week."

She smoothed her silk dress down and literally swayed her way out of my office.

Anything else would have to wait till another time.

I needed to see if there was anyone in the UK I could visit for a chat.

CHAPTER SIX

The next day in my office I started leafing through the crumpled address book. I noted that many addresses were actually not included and as it turned out, a lot of the numbers were 'unobtainable'. Then I got lucky on Paul Belling; it was ringing.

"Hello is that Paul Belling?" I asked as somebody lifted the receiver on the other end.

"Yes, who is this?" a small voice answered rather hesitatingly.

"I'm sorry to bother you but my name is Charlie Moray, I'm trying to get in touch with Wayne Saunders...."

Before I could continue the phone went down.

Did I get cut off, or was that intentional?

I tried the number again but this time it just rang.

That was interesting, I thought but dismissed it as just one of those things.

Under "G" was a woman's name, Gloria Transom in South London. The phone rang for a while until a soft voice answered.

I introduced myself and then followed with my line that I wanted to get in touch with Wayne Saunders.

"Why, has he died?" she retorted in a clipped tongue.

"Not that I know of, Miss Transom," I replied caught off balance.

"Then why are you calling? I haven't heard from him for years. Does he owe you money too?"

And then it dawned on her.

"How did you get my number?" she now sounded a little nervous.

"Please don't be concerned, his mother has been in touch and ….

The phone went down.

This was getting a little repetitive. *Was it mentioning Wayne or his mother that was ending any conversations*?

Also under "G" was Guy Robertson, the friend Diana Saunders had mentioned. By the side of his name were two interlocking male symbols (⚣). I didn't feel it was rocket science to work that one out: a homosexual probably.

This time there was an address in Pelynt in Cornwall. I decided to make this the last call of the day and it turned out to be a turning point.

I got through to Guy. At first, like the others, he was reluctant to chat but as I slowly won his trust, he seemed almost eager to get the records straight.

He was a good friend of Wayne. In fact, he said that they lived together for a while in San Francisco. From there they had moved to Los Angeles and were an item for some time. He said that even though they did eventually split up, they had stayed in touch sporadically over the years.

Guy was genuinely concerned to know how Wayne was getting on but once again, the mention of Diana Saunders brought the conversation almost to a halt.

I was pretty desperate to get some understanding about Wayne, the man himself, by someone who knew him as well as Guy obviously did.

Before I lost this contact over the phone, I wanted to assure him that I was genuinely interested to also get the record straight and suggested I come and meet him in Plymouth. I really was prepared to travel down by train to meet him.

Fortunately he agreed and we made a date to meet.

Before very long, I would discover that Diana Saunders was after more than just her money back.

She wanted her pound of flesh too!

CHAPTER SEVEN

The train arrived in Plymouth and I didn't have to look far for Guy Robertson who said he would be over by the ticket office. It's safe to say that the tall, blonde, blue-eyed man standing there was undeniably a friend of Wayne. Guy Robertson was one handsome looking man, even to my heterosexual self.

The thought struck me that Wayne and Guy must have looked quite a stunning pair in their youth; A couple tailor-made for the Hollywood silver screen.

I approached Guy, and with a strong handshake, I introduced myself. I felt this was a good start to our meeting.

"I've booked a restaurant over by the harbour," Guy said with a smile that must have set him back a few thousand. "Nice view where the odd large yacht can be seen and a good view of Drake's Island."

"Sounds good to me," I said and we headed for the Restaurant. It was just a short distance from the station. We arrived and were led to a nice table overlooking the harbour. There were yachts moored there that I could only dream of owning.

In between exchanging choices over the menu, I showed Guy Wayne's address book and asked him if he knew what the symbols were in it. He grinned and said there was always a time when being homosexual was something to hide and this was a way of identification and a bit of self-preservation. It was as I had thought that the 2 male symbols, indeed signified male homosexuals. In short, it was a way of protecting themselves and he added that they also had a language, Polari, which homosexual men could use to survive the slings and arrows thrown at them by the ignorant, not to mention the law.

"Bona to vada your dolly old eek!" he said suddenly.

I hoped he wasn't being rude and laughed. Before I could guess what he had said...

"Good to see your nice face," he laughed knowingly.

This introduction eased me into our meeting and I found Guy a very easy-going person and I hoped he might be a good lead to Wayne's whereabouts.

That thought went out the window, however, when Guy repeated that he hadn't been in touch with Wayne for a while. He might have an old address but he would need to be assured Wayne was happy to be found, especially knowing his mother was sending a Detective to find him.

I decided to stop delving for his address and have a lighter conversation and perhaps reveal a bit about Wayne's journey from America and ultimately Hollywood.

As our starters arrived, I began with the usual question.

"How did you know and meet Wayne?"

"They were good times, you know," Guy responded with a distant smile. "We were physically in the greatest shape and in demand. I met him on a modelling assignment for *Physique Pictorial*."

Apparently, this was one of the ways in which to earn good money and get into the 'movies'.

I was intrigued as to how long it had taken Wayne to be discovered.

"It's not what you know, it's who you know and Wayne was very good at networking to his advantage," Guy revealed. "He was spotted in *Physique Pictorial* by a chap named Raymond Quincy and became his muse, so to speak."

Guy then offered to show me some of the paintings with an invitation to go back to his hotel.

"Come up and see his etchings!" he offered with a wry smile.

I was to find that the paintings Wayne had posed for were, indeed, his entry into Hollywood. By any stretch of the imagination this was definitely the reason for his popularity as an "extra" in the 'movies'.

I wasn't sure where this Quincy character came onto the scene. He had obviously taken a shine to Wayne and used him in his art work featuring the naked man in erotic poses. Quincy ran a Fine Arts Studio in Los Angeles and it wasn't long before Wayne was a partner in the business as well as in Quincy's bed."

"But it didn't last long," Guy sighed.

"What happened?" I asked.

"Well, there's no fool like an old fool and Quincy was an old fool at least 20 years older than Wayne.   He fell for him hook line and sinker making Wayne his muse and his lover.   Wayne was becoming quite famous starring in so many of Quincy's paintings, like the *Aztec Sacrifice* but then I heard that Wayne got quite greedy and actually ripped the guy off in the end. It all went very sour and in a fit of pique Quincy kicked him out, saying he was a gold digger and scratched his name out on all the stationery they had shared."

This was not boding well for my notes on Wayne. If he ripped one person off, why not his mother?   And didn't she call him a gold digger?

"Wayne and I took up most of our time body building," Guy continued. "Our physique opened doors but Wayne went that bit further and got to know all the Chiefs of Casting. That was his entry into the 'movies' as an 'extra' and the rest, as they say, is history."

At that point, the waiter arrived and took away our plates. We sat back before the main course and relaxed as our wine was poured.

"As for his mother," Guy said unexpectedly, and with some bitterness. "She just couldn't keep out of his life."

Guy shook his head.

It was becoming more and more apparent that Diana Saunders was a constant in Wayne's life and not necessarily a good one.

"Wayne and I had an on/off relationship," Guy continued. "It was quite volatile at times and that's why we called it a day when he moved to LA. He doesn't owe me anything, and I have nothing to lose in telling you what I know about his life whilst we were in touch. I also went to live in Los Angeles for a while and heard through mutual friends what Wayne was getting up to. We went from being a steady relationship to 'just good friends' and occasionally still met up. It suited both of us. I still cared for him and I know he felt the same way. It just didn't work out living together."

Guy continued. "Wayne kept in touch and sent me newspaper clippings from *Screen International* and *Variety* when he got picked for *The Ten Commandments* and the Marilyn Monroe films."

I put down my glass of wine as our main meal arrived. We ate in a comfortable silence, not only digesting the meal but all the things we had talked about.

We were about to order dessert when Guy said that he had been in a slight dilemma as to whether to show me a letter from Wayne's mother. He felt this was not the place for it but wanted to share what he called 'the other side' of Diana Saunders.

Guy suggested we go back to his place to read it. We got the bill and took a cab back to Pelynt. Guy was running a well-established hotel and suggested I book in at "mate's rates" and possibly stay over for as long as necessary. It was a nice invitation and as it was quite late, the thought of getting the train back to London wasn't very tempting.

I took up Guy's kind invitation.

*****

Now in Guy's living room he poured us a glass of wine and went over to his bureau to retrieve the letter.

As he had mentioned earlier, Guy produced some rather erotic photographs which Wayne and he had posed for in *Physique Pictorial*. There was no doubt about it, they both had amazing physiques.

Guy handed me the letter which was in Diana Saunders distinctive handwriting.

As I started to read it Guy was drawn away to the reception area to deal with a client, which gave me time to continue reading the letter and digest its contents.

Dear Guy,

Don't be too surprised to get a letter from me but life is made up of surprises and I had quite a few last week.

The first was that my son has disowned me, but that didn't bother me one little bit but when I got information that he had stolen £10,000 from me, then that was a different matter. Maybe because he has not heard from me that he thinks I have been sitting back breaking my heart because I shall not see him again. On the contrary, I shall be seeing him. I have been in touch with the police and also the bank and I shall soon be in a position to take a warrant out for his arrest.

I intend to have his photograph and quite a column on the front page of a paper so that everybody will see it and by the time I am finished with him he won't even get any work. It will cost him plenty. L.A. won't be big enough to hold him. I have his letters which will help. I shall write to some of his friends and anyone without his address will be able to read all about it. I don't give a damn what mud will be slung, but you can tell Mr Saunders for me, I have a few cards up my sleeve that won't be too healthy for him – he still has time to take the money back to Gibraltar Savings and hand it to Miss Swanson, or send it direct to me, then I shall drop the whole thing – but if this is not forthcoming by the time my investigations are complete, then I shall go ahead.

Any son that is rotten to the core would not rob his mother, had he written and asked me for cash, I would have let him have what he wanted gladly, but to pinch it the way he has done is another matter and he must not be allowed to get away with it regardless – wherever he is I shall get him, the world is small.

Guy returned. I was slightly shocked by the tone of the letter from a mother to a son but decided to read the rest of it another time.

"Take it," Guy said with some sadness. "It has brought me nothing but misery and bad luck, so you're welcome to it. I don't know why I've kept it this long? It's not been a particularly nice link to him."

I felt that Guy had been waiting for an opportunity to share the letter and at last to be able to hand it over. It was almost like the lifting of a curse.

"I've been reluctant to throw it away but something has made me hang on to it," he said pausing thoughtfully.

Guy had not heard from Wayne for some time, and it seemed it was the right decision to let it go.

The letter was a hard read but the more I absorbed the contents, the more I wondered if I would be able to share the experience with Diana Saunders? I had more or less decided I was not going to let her know I had possession of the letter.

"Did you reply?" I asked Guy.

"No, I didn't reply," Guy said.

He said that he didn't know where to start. He had no idea what Wayne had done to extract such venom from his mother. In fact, it wasn't really making a lot of sense. Yes, there was the "stolen" £10,000 but the vitriol about her son was unbelievable.

"It was too awful and I didn't want to be dragged into whatever was going on between Wayne and his mother. As I saw it, she was in his life far too much and perhaps they were very much alike in a way."

It was evident that Guy wanted to remember Wayne as a charming, handsome boyfriend of his. He did admit that Wayne was tight with his money and was drawn towards the rich and the famous.

I was beginning to get an idea of this rather complex man called Wayne, who obviously did very well for himself but left a lot of people by the wayside.

So for that matter did his mother!

CHAPTER EIGHT

It had been a pleasant meeting with Guy. I felt I knew much more about Wayne than I could have possibly found out from his mother. It was getting really late and Guy handed me a key and I went to my room. As I got undressed, the letter from Wayne's mother dropped out of my pocket onto the floor. I picked it up and got into bed. I decided this might make some scary night time reading but it was going to give me a real insight into this woman and her motives.

And so it continued:

I can assure you he can never boast of giving me anything, if he ever spent a penny on me, he got back double. He is so despicable that he even used to talk about me behind my back to my friends, just as he does about his. I never ever told him but it just shows his mentality. I never was very close to him but now he can say what he likes about me. I couldn't care less. I tell you, Guy, I wouldn't even wait to put the cap on him, but I have to wait for certain documents and it takes time. Should be early July. I wonder if he has had any sleepless nights, yet – do you remember when he starred in the psychopathic ward in General Hospital – perhaps they should have taken him to the real place and thrown away the key.

When he came over to England, he hadn't seen Lester for 11 years and Lester did his utmost in his little way to make him as comfortable as he could, and yet when he came back, he hadn't got a good word to say about him and the kids, actually he is not fit to clean his brother's boots. I left a little money from his father's life insurance to Lester and told him that he was at liberty to use it if needed – I can assure you, Guy, there were times when Lester was hard pressed but that money was never even touched – that's the difference in the 2 brothers.

I can give you his character, looking back in the past I really shouldn't be surprised at anything he would stoop to. I am talking with a news telecaster and this will kill Wayne. He is going to regret this for the rest of his life. I do not intend to stop at anything, as I am getting considerable help from the other side and nobody will ever look at him again, believe me.

I am sorry I have had to do this Guy, but I do want to give him an opportunity to save himself and if I get no satisfaction soon, then I shall give the word GO.

I do hope life is kind to you, Guy, and I would like to hear from you – maybe I can tell you something to your advantage.
My kindest regards, Diana Saunders

After reading to the end, I was more convinced than ever that this wasn't just an attempt on Diana's part to get her money back.

The wine had helped earlier but I still fell into a rather troubled sleep.

The following morning I made my way down to the dining room, where Guy was already busily helping out with the breakfast and chatting to diners. My train was booked for late afternoon back to Paddington, but I was hoping to have a little more time with Guy.

At the end of breakfast, Guy said it was a busy time but he could spend an hour with me if there was anything else that came to mind. I felt comfortable enough to show Guy the address book, especially as he could identify the symbols as well. Perhaps he could recognise some of the names that would help my investigation.

I asked him if he knew about someone called Rita. At this, Guy was slightly evasive but did admit to having met her once.

"All I will tell you is, that Wayne is not in England," Guy said with real empathy. "He's definitely still over in the States, but I am telling you this in confidence as I don't want to be party to his mother finding him."

This was going to be difficult as my investigation was precisely that; to find him and let his mother know where he was.

"I really can't tell you more, as you have not yet discovered how wicked his mother can be; the letter is just a taster of what she is really like. He wouldn't thank me for leading his mother to him."

Now I had a dilemma.

CHAPTER NINE

I got my afternoon train back to Paddington station.

My visit to Guy needed to be kept quiet but I thought I might need to take another trip to Plymouth at some later date.

I went back to my office deep in thought, with so much information on my mind. I felt a headache coming on.

I phoned Mrs Saunders to let her know that I had taken a trip to Plymouth but decided to lie about my meeting with Guy and tell her that he had very little to say and was not a good contact.

However, it was Geraldine, the maid, who happened to pick up the phone.

"Mrs Saunders is not in," she said politely.

"Geraldine, it's Detective Moray here," I said. "Is there any chance we could meet up? I know you don't want to say too much but I do want to hear more about Wayne. I've met one of his friends, Guy. Believe me, it was most instructive and I promise I won't tell Mrs Saunders just what Guy and I have discussed."

I heard her take a sharp intake of breath down the phone line. The moment's pause seemed to last an eternity.

"I just want to know that Wayne is alright and he knows I'm thinking of him," she said quietly.

"Geraldine, anything you say to me will be in confidence." I almost pleaded, hoping she would believe me. "Perhaps you might want to think about it and call me another time."

I gave her my number and tried to emphasise that I too was concerned about Wayne. In fact, it wasn't too far from the truth. I was beginning to see another side to this case thanks to Wayne's address book.

"I'll think about it," she said.

She added that she'd tell Mrs Saunders I had called and abruptly hung up.

CHAPTER TEN

If Wayne was still in touch with Geraldine, I needed to keep in touch with her. She obviously was more than just an important bystander in the home. Geraldine's concern for Wayne was quite touching and she had been in the employ of the Saunders since her youth. Geraldine knew something and I had to get to the bottom of her life with the family, as her reaction to my questions was very protective towards Wayne.

At the same time, Geraldine seemed rather nervous around Mrs Saunders, almost frightened. I began to wonder what Diana may have on Geraldine, or perhaps she was scared for another reason. Geraldine would be a work in progress and I would have to tread very carefully with her, as she may well prove the key to Wayne's whereabouts after all.

I also thought that Geraldine might well have some insight into the relationship of the two brothers. I wanted to get in touch with Lester but I needed to get the timing right. I knew Mrs Saunders wasn't keen and really the brothers seemed to be quite estranged from each other. This was a pity. Mind you, there was also Lester's wife, Hannah. I could imagine she had some stories to tell.

When Lester was struggling financially they all lived together under his mother's roof and her controlling rules. This must have been quite uncomfortable for Hannah even before the kids came along. According to Diana Saunders, Lester's fortunes improved and the family eventually moved out but perhaps not far enough; only a few streets away. This way Diana could continue to exercise control over Lester, while Wayne at least had escaped to America.

I opened up the notebook and wondered if the hieroglyphics might be a shorthand that could be recognised by none other than my old secretary, Gloria. She was with me in the good old days when they were almost queuing for my services.

I decided to give her a call.

"Hi Gloria, it's Charlie here, sorry it's been a while." I ventured.

"You can say that again," she responded sarcastically. "I'm still waiting for my gold watch from you. I suppose you want something. What's up?" she blurted out at canon speed.

I asked her if she had time to pop over and take a look at the notebook and see if the hieroglyphics were indeed, some form of shorthand.

"I've got nothing better to do today," she said with a sigh. "If you're around in the next hour, I'll pop over to the office."

I was so relieved as I didn't really want to give the book to anyone I didn't trust.

"Great!" I responded with a laugh. "I'll be here, waiting for you as usual!"

"You'd better be," was her curt reply.

While I waited for Gloria, I continued to look through the notebook.

I needed to write to the Navy for information on Wayne, as going by his notebook, he had spent a good deal of time during the war aboard various British Navy ships. At least I would be able to find out from his records which places he may have visited and what his job was on board.

I realised I should have visited the Naval base in Portsmouth. I didn't have the time to go from Portsmouth to Plymouth on my visit to Guy Robertson. I put it on my 'to do' list for now to see if it was worth making a special visit and drop in on the base direct from London.

I put the notebook down and flicked through the address book.

I started to think of the contacts I needed to make apart from the Navy. Perhaps *Screen International* or even *Variety* might turn up something on Wayne Saunders' career in the pictures. There was always the rich and famous. His mother did say he had been rubbing shoulders with Marilyn Monroe. Perhaps as an extra he may not be credited but it was worth checking out.

There was a knock at the door and true to form there was Gloria, standing poised with her hands on her hips, punctual as ever. I was so pleased to see her.

"Well, let's get down to it, the clock's ticking and I charge a lot more for my work than when you last saw me!" she said with a sly smile, "at least double nothing," she joked.

I laughed as I handed her the notebook.

She looked through nodding and confirmed it was Pitman's shorthand in part and could make out a fair bit of the writing. She asked if she could take it away and do it.

"I'd rather you worked on it here," I confessed, "I don't really want it to leave my side."

"It might take a few days, you know," she frowned. "There's a fair bit here and the writing's not too clever in places."

"Agreed," I nodded.

She went over to her desk and before long the ever diligent Gloria had gone to work on the notebook as if she had never left.

*****

Gloria wasted no time and it was nice to hear the soft sound of fingers hitting keys on the typewriter in the background.

Meanwhile, I started looking at back issues of *Screen International* and *Variety*. "What a list," I muttered.

It began with the 1952 version of '*The Ten Commandments*' with Yul Brynner and Charlton Heston. There was also a reference to '*Gentlemen Prefer Blondes*' with Marilyn Monroe. Wayne had definitely got in with the right crowd. He may well have been just an 'Extra' but it looked as though he was never out of work.

"Hey Gloria," I shouted, "his mum did say he was in a couple of Marilyn Monroe pictures, so at least she did tell some truth."

"Nice for him," Gloria shouted back.

"Just like old times isn't it." I said with genuine affection.

"Yeah," she said. "It is. All work and no pay."

"No," I assured her. "This client's fairly loaded and I was even given an advance," I boasted. "You'll even get expenses."

"I'll believe it when I see it," she said knowingly.

"Oh ye of little faith," I replied chuckling.

My mind was doing overtime looking through the list of pictures Wayne had starred in. I was interested to find out how he got so well into the Hollywood scene.

I needed to get a letter off to the film studios; Paramount and 20th Century Fox to see if Wayne might still be working at either of them.

"Interesting bloke, this Wayne," Gloria was working steadily through the notebook.

"He mentions a brother but I can't make out his name."

"Lester," I replied helpfully.

"Oh yes, that works. Listen to this…
Had a fight last night with Lester. Good punch up. Ma broke us up. I got thumped by her as

usual. He writes *Ma* a lot instead of Mother. *Dad got arrested*."

"That sounds about right," I replied. "His Dad had a gambling club of sorts."

"Hooray, joined the Navy," Gloria continued. *"Ma didn't see me off - typical. What's that about*, I thought.

Saddest day of my life. Only Geraldine cares."

Gloria looked up at me. "Who's this Geraldine?"

"She's the maid." Then it struck me that my instincts were right; Wayne and Geraldine had a connection.

"He joined the Navy and looks like he was a Writer, a Scribe," Gloria added.

I thought that made sense as his way of writing was very clear and made interesting reading.

Gloria volunteered to do a few more pages before leaving and left me to continue looking at the list of pictures Wayne had starred in. It was turning out that he rubbed shoulders with some of the greats. Lloyd Bridges, Yul Brynner, Marilyn Monroe, John Wayne, Debra Paget, Jane Russell.

"Time to go." Gloria stopped typing abruptly and picked up her bag. "I can pop in tomorrow about 10 for a few hours, if that suits?"

"Oh, that would be great," I replied, genuinely relieved that she was going to return so quickly.

"Fancy dropping in to *The Crown* for a drink and a catch up before you go home?"

"Yeah, why not? I'll give my old man a ring and let him know, you're paying me in kind!" Gloria smiled mischievously. She put her coat on and we both left the office laughing in the way we used to when the world didn't seem so complicated.

"It's been a good day's work after all," we agreed.

CHAPTER ELEVEN

Another booking from Physique Pictorial. Lunch with Guy. Met Raymond Quincy. Interesting lunch. Visited Liberace today, even saw his closets…!

Gloria was cutting through the notebook, like a hot knife through butter.

It was proving to be a real guide and insight into Wayne's life and was producing several leads I could follow up myself.

Then the phone rang. Gloria picked it up automatically.

"Good morning, Moray's Agency," she chimed. "How can I help you?"

"Who's that?" was the sharp retort back.

"I'm Mr Moray's secretary," Gloria stated.

"Would you like to speak to him? He is here. Who should I say is calling?"

"Tell him it's Mrs Diana Saunders."

Gloria covered the receiver but I had already heard Mrs Saunders hectoring voice.

I took the phone from her.

"Hello, Mrs Saunders." I breezed. "How are things?"

"I heard you phoned," she accused. "You didn't have a secretary when I last saw you at your office." Diana Saunders sounded as if she was in interrogation mode and I was on the receiving end.

"I know," I explained, "but what with the volume of information in that notebook, I needed someone I could trust to go through it and translate the shorthand.

"I see." She was intrigued.

"And did you find anything of interest?"

"Not really," I lied. But there are some contacts I'd like to follow up, mainly in the States.

"Oh right," she said. Then changed her tone. "So you met Guy then?"

Again I hesitated anxious to get my script right.

"Yes, we met but he hasn't been in touch with Wayne for over a year," I said at last. "He didn't have an address for him."

"That's rather strange as they were *very* close, if you know what I mean," she continued, clearly not believing me and digging still deeper.

"It was a long way to go for very little information but I can't help feeling that Guy might be hiding something," I continued, hoping it came out convincingly. "Perhaps another visit might be useful or maybe a phone call just to build up some trust."

"I suppose so," she responded. Clearly disappointed that I hadn't come back with more. "Are you really sure Guy didn't say anything about him?"

"He spoke about how they met and that they got into the 'movies' around the same time but he wouldn't offer anything to indicate that they were still in touch," I continued, eager to change the subject.

"I'm thinking of visiting the Naval base in Portsmouth to check out his records."

"What good will that do?" she snapped. "I can't imagine the British Navy give a hoot about Wayne Saunders and any paperwork on him will be minimal, if anything at all. I think you're on a hiding to nothing following that kind of lead and wasting my money on a few days holiday in Portsmouth. I think you'd be better off calling up some of the names in the address book in America."

I was beginning to get the distinct impression that she really knew where Wayne was living but just went along with her suggestion.

"I agree," Mrs Saunders, I said. "If Wayne's still alive, and there's no proof that he isn't, the place to find him is America. But America's a big place, Mrs Saunders, so I need to talk to a few of the contacts in his address book first."

There was a sullen silence at the end of the phone. Clearly this wasn't going the way Diana had hoped.

"One person I still haven't spoken to is Wayne's brother, Lester," I ventured.

"Are you sure Lester isn't in touch with him? I would like to meet up with him if that's possible?"

The sullen silence continued. I imagined her painted face frowning at the other end of the line.

"They were nothing like each other," she snapped at last. "Lester is a decent man, works hard and has a lovely family. Not like Wayne, the little scroat, he was always selfish, that's probably why he never married. I don't even think they kept in touch that much; they had nothing in common."

I started to wonder whether she was putting me off because Lester might know something.

"I suppose it can't do any harm," she relented. "But let me call him in advance to tell him you'll be in touch. Make sure he knows I'm trying to contact Wayne as a mother trying to find her son, what with losing touch after all these years."

The tone was false. It seemed a vain attempt to show some maternal instinct and failed miserably.

"Of course," was my instant reply.

I was pleased she couldn't see my own face screwed up in disgust as it was.

CHAPTER TWELVE

Gloria was back in the office at 10 sharp the next morning, diligently working her way through the notebook. She was obviously finding it quite enthralling.

"Oh my goodness, Charlie, he met Cecil B de Mille," she said at one point. "It was obviously important as he spelt the name out."

"Yes," I replied. "It seems he knew a lot of Hollywood celebrities."

Gloria looked up as if something had just occurred to her. "You don't think Wayne could have been caught up in anything more serious if he was mixing with this lot?" she asked after a while.

There were times when Gloria was a bit more than a secretary and this was one of them.

The idea that Wayne had been sucked into the vortex, into a bigger intrigue in

Hollywood had not crossed my mind until this point.

Now my brain cells were racing in overtime. I was still following this train of thought when the phone rang.

"Moray."

"Hello, Detective Moray?" a good strong voice sounded down the end of the phone. "This is Lester Saunders here."

The caller caught me on the hop. I hadn't expected him to reply so soon.

"My mother says you want to speak to me," Lester continued. "I'm not sure if I've got much more to tell you as Wayne and I haven't really been in touch for some years now. To tell the truth we didn't really have much in common even as youngsters. During the war I was in the Airforce and he was in the Navy. You can't get more apart than that."

Lester was proving much more forthcoming for a first phone call than I had expected, so I didn't interrupt.

"All I can tell you is that he fell out with Ma over a fair bit of money. Quite honestly, I didn't get too involved in that one," he continued. "I know that Ma was very upset with Wayne and it seemed to cause a rift between them. At some point they stopped corresponding."

I thought that was putting it mildly.

"What was he like then?" I ventured, changing tact and hoping to keep the conversation going.

"Well he was always great at telling stories," Lester replied. "Just ask my kids!"

"Would you mind if I came and visited and had a fuller chat," I suggested. "It will help me form a picture of what was going on. You might even know some people over in the States that I could contact."

"I can certainly look for addresses of various family members who live in the States," he said in a friendly and pleasant way. "There were definitely contacts that Wayne was in touch with when he first went out there."

We made a date for a couple of days later.

"Come round to my house as it'll be easier to dig out the family letters if there are any lying around," Lester added.

At last I felt I was moving ahead with the investigation. We made a date and time in the evening as Lester was working.

"See you around six o'clock if that sounds good for you," I said.

"Great, see you then," replied Lester and hung up.

Gloria looked up from her notebook and gave me a knowing smile.

CHAPTER THIRTEEN

I got into the office and found Gloria busily at work like an archaeological scholar deciphering the hieroglyphics in the notebook.

"I've found something really interesting here, which I think you need to follow up if you get round to writing to the Navy base," she said at last. "This is before Liberace and the stuff I translated earlier. I'm definitely into his life in the Navy. I wonder if he would have told Lester?"
In the notebook Wayne had written: *Ironside Corsairs of 1830 Squadron lost crew*.

It certainly sounded interesting but I doubted it was anything that Wayne would have discussed with his brother. They had already gone their separate ways in the Navy and the Airforce, respectively. However, it was worth asking the question.

The day went by without much more happening, except for the odd gasp from Gloria and statements like "you'll never believe this" and "guess what, he got sick again." Gloria laughed. "Couldn't have been much of a sailor," she added with a chuckle.

"He seemed to get around a bit. Here's something about the Suez Canal."

Entry reads: HMS Illustrious. Squeezed through Suez Canal. Saudi Arabia side desolate. Egyptian side busy. World War One monuments and odd-shaped barges 'Dhows'. Moved into Red Sea. Stopped at Aden for refuelling. Next stop Trincomalee, Ceylon.

"Keep going Gloria." I said. "I think his notebook was probably something he was going to use for a possible publication, as he sounds like quite an accomplished writer."

Eventually the clock got round to 5.30pm. Gloria had left earlier and I started getting myself together to visit Lester.

*****

It was pouring with rain when I arrived outside Lester's house in Robson Avenue, Willesden. It was a nice road and the houses looked neat and well kept.

I rang the bell. The door was opened by a tall, smiling and good looking man who welcomed me in. He looked better than the photographs I had from his mother.

"Come on in Detective Moray," he said. "It's rainin' 'eavens 'ard, that's what my Dad used to say."

"Cheers, please call me Charlie," I offered and Lester reciprocated, cutting through the formalities.

With the greetings sorted, Lester led me into the front room.

"Would you like some tea?" he asked.

"That would be great, thanks," I replied.

He left the room and called out.

"Hannah love, come here a second," he shouted. I want you to meet Detective Moray, Charlie."

It was no exaggeration to say that the lady that entered was truly lovely and had an elegance about her.

"This is my wife, Hannah," Lester smiled proudly, "all the way from the kitchen!"

"Nice to meet you," Hannah said with a beautiful smile.

"I'll just make some tea. Would you like something to eat with it?"

"Oh don't go to too much trouble," I said, hoping she would make something anyway.

"It's no bother," she replied. "Lester has just got in from work, so he'll have a snack right now, won't you darling?" Lester nodded and Hannah left the room to make the tea.

"Hannah is from India, you know," he explained. "It's a long story but we met when I was posted in Calcutta. It was a tradition for the

Jewish airmen to get sorted out with a family during our stay and mine was with Hannah's family. Well, the rest is history. I just couldn't leave her behind. We got married there and had our first child in India before coming back to the UK."

"So the Airforce was well worth joining!" I laughed.

"You can say that again," Lester added ruefully. "She was in the films with her sister and they went by the names of Ramola and Ruplekha. Her sister, Ramola was quite famous but my Hannah wasn't quite so keen on being a star. Looking back though, it's a shame that any films she was in, were destroyed during the bombings in India."

"Does she miss India," I enquired.

"Probably more than she says," he replied wistfully. "She's from a family of 4 sisters and today received some very sad news. I would like to be in a position where we could take a holiday and she could visit her family again."

I didn't have a chance to ask what the sad news was about before being suddenly aware of voices coming down the stairs.

Three children appeared inquisitive to know who had arrived.

"Here they are," Lester announced, also with a degree of pride. "This is where my hard-earned money ends up."

He introduced them one by one.

"Daniel, Sarah and Leah; Our littlest, Tina, is upstairs hopefully sleeping, although with the racket they've been making I'm not so sure. I'll just pop up and check."

As Lester went out, Hannah came in with tea and sandwiches and ushered the children out to the kitchen to eat their dinner before going to bed.

"Sorry about the disturbance," Hannah said in her lilting accent.

"No trouble at all, and thanks for the tea and sandwiches," I said really grateful to stop my stomach rumbling. "Really delicious."

Hannah hesitated a while before making a passing comment.

"Have you heard from Wayne at all?" she ventured. "Last time we saw him was a few years ago when he left the Navy. Sadly he didn't stay long and there wasn't much time to get to know him, especially with his mother around."

This set me thinking but before I could follow this line of enquiry, Lester re-entered the room.

"Tina is fast asleep," he announced to Hannah. "Oh lovely, thanks for the tea darling, looks great. Lester winked jokingly as he poured the tea. "I'll be mum he joked."

We settled down and it was Lester that started what was going to be a real eye-opener on the relationship between the two brothers. It also provided some insight into the influence their mother exercised on the whole family.

"Before Wayne and I joined up for the services, I remember one particular evening during a heavy night's blitz," he said. "The noise of the enemy planes and ack-ack fire was particularly loud. You could see the searchlights trying to spotlight the enemy planes and this seemed to fascinate Wayne. I told him to get away from the window and go to bed, or I'd put him in bed; that was all that was needed for us to end up having a real fist fight and trying to punch the living daylights out of each other. Our yelling and screaming was so loud it drowned out the constant din of the anti-aircraft guns and Ma came bursting into the room. I'm laughing now but we did need someone to separate the two of us before we did some lasting damage to each other. It was our Dad that eventually split us up but Wayne got a real tongue lashing from Ma."

"Did you fight often?" I asked.

"Not really", Lester replied after a moment's hesitation. "That said, that particular night Wayne seemed really bothered about something."

"I think he was planning to leave home but we never really discussed things. In hindsight, it was a bit sad I suppose. I left home before him and Ma and Dad saw me off but by all accounts Wayne went to the railway station himself, so he must have felt quite bad – must have been hard; never really thought about it before."

"Did you keep in touch while you were away?" I asked.

"I would send telegrams and letters to Ma," Lester continued. "I knew she'd get a kick out of receiving notes from abroad."

At that moment Hannah came in to ask if we wanted any more tea.

"No thank you," I said. "It was all very nice. Good to meet you both and the children."

It was getting late and I felt it was time to call it a night.

"Oh just a minute," Lester responded, "I've found some photographs you might like to see. Wayne and some celebrities you might recognise. He sent these at the beginning when he starred in *The Ten Commandments* and then later in *No Business, Like Show Business*, with Marilyn Monroe. He wanted to share how well he was getting on; but then the letters stopped shortly after. I know we didn't touch on it but around that time was when the money exchanged hands and Ma was not happy with him."

I don't think she was ever happy with him," Hannah chipped in nervously.

Lester looked round quite aghast.

"Why did you say that?" he demanded.

"Because she's never happy unless she gets the attention." Hannah said, her voice shaking with conviction.

"Oh honey, that's a bit harsh," Lester was getting a bit edgy.

Hannah looked at him, then turned to me.

"Nice to meet you anyway," she said and went back towards the kitchen.

"Sorry if I've hit a nerve," I said as contritely as I could. I didn't really know what else to say.

"That's OK," Lester said, "It's been a tough day today for Hannah. She received a telegram to say that her father had passed away. It's not the greatest way to receive that sort of news. There's no time for her to get to India, even if we could afford it. To tell the truth it's been hard for her as she hasn't seen her folks since the kids were born. That's a long time not to see your parents, and now it's too late to see her Dad."

I could tell he was saying this with some feeling.

"I'm really sorry to hear that," I answered quickly. "Let's call it a night and meet up another time if that's OK with you."

I got up to leave but felt I needed at least to acknowledge Hannah and pay my respects.

"Do you mind if I just say goodbye to Hannah?" I felt quite bad not knowing the circumstances but Lester hadn't warned me, so I was none the wiser when I arrived.

I went into the kitchen and was shocked to see that she had been crying. I didn't know her but I was very moved by this little, gentle lady who had left her own family behind and was now never to see her father again.

As I approached her to offer my condolences, she addressed me quietly.

"Find Wayne and warn him that his mother is looking for him," she said holding my gaze.

Lester walked in and Hannah went silent. I said my goodbyes and that I was sorry it was such bad timing but I hoped it would be possible to meet again.

When I stood outside, the rain had stopped.

CHAPTER FOURTEEN

The next morning, I got to the office having thought about the meeting with Lester and Hannah. I was still thinking about the 'warning' Hannah made before I left.

Just a quick glance told me that Gloria's translating was coming along nicely.

I love trifle. I'll never have a cup of tea in my life again. Near hit. House shook. Joined the Navy. Ma furious. I don't care. Geraldine upset – gave me a St. Christopher.

Got arrested. Geraldine paid bail. Back to Navy, hooray!

What is religion but a pain in the arse. Got sick again. Is it a sin to be circumcised?!

Sad day. Another Corsair and pilot did not return. Ironside has done a blinder.

I noted the entry about Geraldine and wondered what made her pay bail for Wayne. I hoped she would eventually call.

***

I got interested in further investigating the regular entries about the Corsair plane and found it was one of the Navy's secret weapons. Wayne seemed quite fascinated by this aircraft and there were a number of entries made aboard the aircraft carrier, HMS Illustrious. Landing and taking off was extremely difficult. A catapult technique was employed to launch the aircraft and arresting wires were used on its landing. A hook would catch on to a wire on the landing strip and would help the plane to slow down and land on the short runway without running off the end of the ship.

It was evident it required top class pilots with nerves of steel to be able to take off and land on the ship.

CHAPTER FIFTEEN

As if my thoughts were answered, the following day, just as I got in the office, the phone rang. I picked it up to hear this quiet nervous voice, which I immediately identified as Geraldine.

"I'm leaving in an hour on the Flying Scotsman," she announced. "Can you meet me at A1 Milk Bar on the King's Cross Road at 10.30?"

It was already 9.00am. Fortunately I had no other plans and my curiosity would have cancelled any plans anyway.

"Of course, Geraldine," I said grabbing my briefcase. "I'm leaving right now. I'll see you at the café. I know where it is. I'll be there as soon as I can."

"OK," the quiet voice replied and hung up.

I dashed off to the station.

*****

The lone figure of Geraldine sat in the coffee shop in the remotest corner of the bar. She was hugging a cup of coffee that she had long since finished.

"Hello Geraldine, can I get you something?" I asked gently.

She shook her head and looked down. I could see she was extremely anxious. I was also getting quite anxious as time was ticking on. I would have to work swiftly to put her at ease, otherwise I was going to lose this valuable insight into Wayne's life.

"Geraldine you have my word that I will say nothing to Mrs Saunders," I pleaded with all the sincerity I could muster. "Anything you say to me will be in total confidence."

"Mrs Saunders," she responded bitterly. "The only reason I'm talking to you, Detective Moray, is because I've made a decision to leave

Mrs Saunders. I'm going to Scotland to stay with my sister and believe me I'm not coming back."

Geraldine hesitated for several seconds before continuing.

"I can't tell you everything," she almost breathed the words. "It's just too horrible."

"What's too horrible?" I coaxed her with some concern.

"I just can't say but please believe me, I am worried for Wayne." She seemed to be holding back tears.

"He knows something which is the real reason his mother wants to find him."

This was quite a revelation. I was really intrigued by her response but given her agitated state, I had to give my softly-softly approach.

"What can you tell me about Wayne?" I soothed hoping to diffuse her concerns.

"We would look out for each other, Wayne and me," she said and then paused. "There were times when Lester and Mrs

Saunders were out and Wayne and I would sit in the kitchen and do jigsaw puzzles. One particular night I was sitting in the kitchen and Wayne had gone to his bedroom. The next thing I felt was his hands covering my eyes. Wayne told me to turn round slowly and open them."

Geraldine was speaking with a little more confidence. Perhaps, at last, I would find the real reason for Wayne's departure to America.

"He was standing there with his brother's RAF uniform on," Geraldine said after a while. "He looked fantastic. He desperately wanted to wear the uniform even though he still had another year to go before he would have his own uniform in the Navy. He looked amazing, standing there in front of me. He had really grown. He wasn't 17 yet, but he looked old enough to be in the service."

There was clearly genuine pride in Geraldine's voice.

"Lester and Wayne got on quite well most of the time," Geraldine continued. "But Wayne always felt that Lester got all the attention."

"According to Wayne's diary he and Lester had a really big fight one night," I coaxed.

"They really beat each other up." Geraldine admitted. "That said, although Lester was told off, he didn't have to clear up the mess. In fact, Wayne didn't only have to clear up the mess but his mother took his week's wages."

"I see," I said.

"Mrs Saunders didn't seem to notice Wayne sometimes," Geraldine shook her head sadly.

"There were times when he was very depressed and even spoke of feeling suicidal."

It seemed that Wayne's attempts to get into the Navy, even though he was underage, continued until he was so desperate he decided to break the news that he had joined.

"I had made his favourite trifle but he wasn't eating and his mother was getting really ratty with him. She asked him what the matter was. He just came out with it. *I joined the Navy today, Ma.*"

Geraldine looked down and checked her watch.

Time was ticking by.

"You would have thought he had told his mother he had killed someone," she continued. "Mrs S went mad. She called him all sorts of names, '*you little urchin*' and worse. He told her again, '*I joined the Navy.*' This time his voice was really quiet but firm. His mother told him he wasn't old enough and she was going to tell his father."

Geraldine seemed to remember this quite vividly.

"Wayne mustered up as much strength as he could and told her, '*They lowered the age group*,'" Geraldine continued. "I knew this was a lie. It was the first time Wayne had not only lied to his mother but didn't back down. To start with Mrs Saunders acted really strangely and just carried on eating. But like a volcano only with a mouth full of trifle, she exploded at him and told him he was an ungrateful little bastard – Geraldine looked to the floor guiltily. "I'm sorry for saying such a word," she continued, "but his mother was so spiteful. She said she would be well rid of him and the Navy were welcome to him – perhaps make a man out of him.   It was so awful. I had to clear the dishes but could still hear her shouting at him from the kitchen."

Geraldine took a breather.

"You know something, I think I need a cup of coffee after all."

I went over to the counter and ordered our coffees.   When I returned she had broken down in tears.

"It just hurts to speak about it," she sobbed. "I hope you understand."

I really felt for this little Irish lady who so obviously had a great deal of compassion for Wayne. It was very evident she had quietly defended him his whole life.

With more than a little guilt I realised this was upsetting her but I needed to get her 'take' on the real Wayne. The more I heard about him, the more I wanted to find him. I just hadn't made up my mind why, yet.

The waitress broke the atmosphere as coffee arrived.

Geraldine then continued to speak about that night when Wayne had made his announcement.

"As you can imagine, it was an emotional evening," she said. "Wayne was that desperate to leave home. I remembered he had cried several nights whilst scheming and planning to leave. I went to his room to see if he was alright and put my arms round him and begged him to stay." Geraldine's eyes welled up to the brim once more.

"Mrs Saunders burst into the room absolutely fuming and started accusing me of all sorts," she cried. "The wicked cow made me feel ashamed of myself. Wayne was trying to stick up for me but Mrs Saunders cut him short by shouting at me to *Get out of the house*!"

With trembling fingers Geraldine took a sip of her coffee and then looked at me through her tear stained eyes.

"I should have left then and not come back," she continued, "but it was difficult to get work and I returned the following day, half expecting to be told to leave. Mrs Saunders came to the door and acted as if nothing had happened, so I continued working there until today."

This stirring up of events had made her take stock of everything and indeed, to question why she was still working for Mrs Saunders.

"Wayne got arrested once and they were going to let him just rot in jail," Geraldine said almost by way of confessional. "Awful it was, I paid his bail in the end. It wasn't long after that Mr Saunders died."

"I heard he had a heart attack," I mentioned, in the hope of Geraldine opening up a bit.

There was a silence that followed which spoke volumes of some dreaded incident that may well have taken place but I couldn't reach. Geraldine had hidden it deep in her mind, in the hope she wouldn't have to face it again.

Mrs Saunders said he had a heart attack," she breathed with an utter lack of conviction.

Geraldine glanced down at her watch again anxiously.

"Please continue," I almost pleaded.

"I won't talk about the funeral, you'll have to ask Wayne."

Then she opened up, at least in part.

CHAPTER SIXTEEN - THE FUNERAL

It was like something out of the pictures, only without the rain. Nonetheless it was bleak and overcast on that cold winter's morning.

If the Funeral Directors were open at midnight my mother would have been first in the queue. It was a hasty funeral. Synagogue subscription paid off. Jewish tradition suggests that a body should be buried as soon as possible after death, even within 24 hours. So no-one was surprised that it was the day after Dad died.

The casket was closed. There was no viewing of the deceased. No autopsy seemed necessary as the coroner signed cause of death: "myocardial infarction".

The congregation were none the wiser. He wasn't a well man, everyone knew that, after all he had been in Shenley for a while as she pointed out on a number of occasions. It was a fast and gentle relief, she had said to the mourners many of whom had lost money at his club. Hannah and two of the children were there. It was a pity that Lester couldn't get leave.

The mourners entered the synagogue. On one side the men in dark suits some with a yarmulke to cover their heads as a sign of respect. On the other side, I caught sight of Geraldine standing alone at the back of the synagogue, with tears in her eyes. Genuine tears, unlike my mother's. The rabbi recited some prayers, gave a good eulogy; such nice things about him which made my mother turn on the waterworks for the congregation to offer words of comfort later on.

Taking the weight of the casket with some of my Dad's closest pals, we carried him to the waiting grave. The procession of mourners followed through to the cemetery. The grave diggers had a brutal job. It was a biting cold day and the feeble winter sun did little to soften the clay.

Ma held my arm tightly at the graveside; there was no-one else to cling to – or so I thought.

She suddenly seemed to become smaller and vulnerable. A little old lady with a small white handkerchief dabbing her eyes and looking downwards towards the casket as it was slowly lowered six feet down. I wondered how she managed to look old or indeed even vulnerable. More prayers were said. The first thud of clay on the lid of the casket.

The Jewish custom is for everyone at the graveside to put two shovels of dirt on the coffin; the first with the shovel upside down to show reluctance to let that person go and the second, the right side up to show acceptance. Ma did two with the shovel the right side up.

Turning to leave, over in the distance behind some gravestones was a tall figure who wasn't family, or could have been a wary friend of my father's. As the congregation moved to leave the grave, Ma made an excuse and moved towards the reluctant figure as though they were one of the accepted mourners. He looked familiar but had his back to the proceedings. He held her for a moment in a comforting hold that looked vaguely familiar.

No-one seemed to notice as she walked back towards the mourners, but I did.

We got in the limousine in silence and returned home to sit, talk, eat and pray according to the Jewish tradition.

It was a good turnout though. No flowers just stones to mark your visit. And ending with everyone wishing all the family a "long life." Something my Dad never got to live.

CHAPTER SEVENTEEN

"They had the funeral but Lester was in the RAF and could not get leave from his post in India." She continued after a while. "Poor Wayne. He had to attend without any real support. I know Mr Saunders hadn't long been out of hospital but Mrs Saunders seemed only too pleased that the poor man had passed on."

Once more she stopped speaking. She clearly thought she had said too much.

"Did you ever see Wayne again after the funeral," I asked, assuming this was when he joined the Navy.

Geraldine shook her head.

"After the funeral I handed Wayne a St. Christopher's medal to protect him and remember me by," she muttered wistfully.

"His departure to join the Navy was so sad. His mother had told him he had ten minutes to pack his things and get out or she would call the police."

The St. Christopher medal clearly meant something to Wayne as it was also referenced in his hieroglyphic notebook.

"So he did join the Navy," I persisted.

"Yes, eventually," she nodded with more sobs. "But he received his honourable discharge after only 6 months, as they found out he was underage and had no alternative but to come back home. Poor thing, he had to work in his father's Club for a while, in fact, off and on, right up until Mr Saunders died."

"Mrs Saunders was ungrateful for the things he brought back for her. She would send him out to the shops for all sorts of things even sanitary products – really disgusting for a man to go and buy."

I guess it would have been fairly embarrassing for a chap, I smiled in agreement.

*****

Without as much as taking a breath she shouted to him, "Wayne, be a good boy and run across the road and get me a large box of sanitary towels from the chemist before the shops close. Lay out the money, I'll give it to you when you get back."

Looking rather sheepish Wayne returned just moments later.

"Hey, Wayne, where are my sanitary towels, where did you put them?" his mother demanded.

Wayne hesitated.

"The chemist was out of them, Ma," he said.

"Out of sanitary towels, never heard of it?" Diana mocked.

She paused then added: "You damn little liar, the Chemist said they have sanitary towels in. What did you tell me a lie for and say they were out of them, huh?"

"Well, I didn't like.. I didn't want… isn't Lester home? Why didn't you ask him to get them for you?" It was uncharacteristic of Wayne to challenge his mother.

"Because I asked you," she seethed.

Jesus Christ, Ma," Wayne almost cried. "I've just come home and already you're starting on me."

*****

We still had time as Geraldine volunteered the full story about Wayne's arrest.

"He was on leave," Geraldine confessed. "One night he got arrested by the police in a compromising situation with a lady of the night and put in the cells."

Geraldine certainly had my attention now.

*****

Wayne dodged into the doorway of a bombed out building to avoid being followed, going smack bang into a woman leaning up against the door. She reeked of cheap but heady and intoxicating perfume. Her hair was long and seductively dyed red. The colour matched her short, tight dress showing off her shapely legs and the tops of her suspenders as she stood in six inch high-heeled shoes.

Above her head hung a sign "Business as Usual".

"'Ere, sailor boy, what's the matter," she coaxed. "Can't you wait a minute before we talk over the matter of price?"

Wayne peered around the side of the doorway. He saw a man in a raincoat seemingly following him.

"'Ow's about a quid for Daisy?" she continued.

Wayne looked at her uneasily and shook his head.

"Now you seem like a nice clean sailor boy, she smiled, 'ow's about 17/6d?"

Wayne's hesitation still egged her on.

"Come up with fifteen bob and you can 'ave me for an hour," she said.

Wayne was still wondering where the man in the raincoat was, when she said:

"Now look, Jack Tar, it's been a rough day, you 'andsome one, you are. Come on, give me 12/6d and let's get with it."

Wayne looked back out the doorway. The man in the raincoat had gone, there was no need to stay.

"Look 'ere, sailor boy, give me ten bob and so 'elp me, gawd, I'm not making a penny on it." She moved in close to Wayne. "Daisy knows all the tricks for 'aving a good time."

She grabbed his arm and turned him around. Pressing her over-developed bosom right into his chest.

"Come on now, sailor, you won't even have to wear a French letter," she let her hand fall slowly and caressingly down over his well-filled out uniform, coming to rest at a pre-determined destination.

"Okay Daisy, get a move on before I take you in." The situation was broken by the sound of a man's voice, and the sight of the raincoat as the man whipped Wayne around.

The man held up a warrant card and Wayne's heart began pounding as he looked up and recognised the face. His heart almost burst. The hours that followed were blurred and indistinct, he was in a police station and signing a statement to the effect that he was wearing the Naval uniform of H.M. Service. Regulations stipulate that service personnel are entitled to dress in their uniform for a period not to exceed thirty days from discharge.

Wayne reached into his jerkin and pulled out a comb. As he did, his identification tags and St. Christopher fell at the feet of the policeman who stooped down and picked them up.

"What's this then, son," he said looking at the St. Christopher as he handed the items back.

"You Catholic, or what?"

"No." Wayne replied. "I'm nothing."

"Oh now come on, you've got to be somethin', the copper mocked as he studied the dog tags. "Sez 'ere on your tags you're Jewish. It also says your name is Saunders. Any relation to Harry Saunders by any chance?"

"He's my father," Wayne replied miserably.

"Cor blimey, 'Arry will kill me if 'e knows I've got you bang to rights." Still laughing, the policeman shook his head.

"Sorry, son, but I got to do this, regulations you know," he sneered in a mocking smile and repeated, . "Old 'Arry will kill me if 'e finds out." His words falling behind him as he left.

*****

Wayne waited in a small dingy cell.

After an eternity, or so it seemed, he heard heavy footfall on the other side of the cell door. The keys rattled, like the chains of Marley's ghost and the door flung open.

It was the same policeman who had arrested him earlier that evening.

"Hello Wayne, how are you?" the policeman smiled falsely.

"Alright, I guess," Wayne moaned.

"Now what's all this about you wearing your uniform?" the Detective continued in a friendly but teasing tone.

"Want to tell me about it?"

"There's nothing to tell," Wayne shrugged. I was discharged from the service 5 or 6 weeks ago and was going out and just decided to wear my uniform. I didn't realise I was doing anything wrong."

"Now, I didn't say you were." The policeman said with a benign grin. "This isn't that serious. How old are you?"

"Seventeen."

"Well then, it's very simple," the policeman continued. We don't want to prefer charges if you weren't doing anything wrong. Where do you live? I'll call your parents and they can come and pick you up. But remember, don't wear your uniform anymore."

"I don't want my parents, Wayne pleaded in despair. I just want to be left alone."

"I'll have to keep you in all night if you don't tell me where you live," the policeman warned. "Now, you don't want that do you?"

"I don't care." Wayne resolutely replied.

"But your Mum and Dad will wonder where you are," he continued, "and you wouldn't want them to worry about you, would you?"

Wayne didn't answer, biting his lower lip with nervousness.

"Now come on son, I haven't got all day."
*The policeman was becoming increasingly
impatient. I'm trying to be nice to you. Where do
you live?"*

*Wayne continued to bite his lip. He
remained silent.*

*"Alright, if you don't tell me, I'll make it my
business to throw the book at you." The
policeman growled. I've tried to be nice but if you
don't play ball I'll have no option but to send you
to prison. How about that, son?"*

Wayne looked at the Detective.

*"I'd rather go to prison than go back
home."*

And so Wayne stayed the night in the cell.
*****

Geraldine picked up the story of how she
had gone to visit him at the police station.

According to his mother, it seemed, a stint in the cell would do him good.

"Wayne was a sorry sight," Geraldine shook her head. "I couldn't leave him there. I decided to pay his bail".

A Hearing was set for the following week at the Probationary Court.

"Mrs Saunders actually came to the Court and saw me with Wayne." Geraldine continued, "She called me a 'good for nothing tramp' and other hurtful names."

Probably much worse I suspected. Geraldine found this shameful and embarrassing.

"Did he get through the court case alright?" I asked.

"It was mainly for wearing the Naval uniform when he wasn't on duty," she explained. Service personnel were only allowed to dress in their uniform for a period not longer than thirty days from discharge. Wayne had been out for over 6 weeks."

"But he got off," I coaxed.

"Yes, he got off but had to return home," Geraldine nodded. "Eventually he got the uniform and did what he wanted to do, which was to join the Navy and most importantly, leave home. Later I found out that his mother didn't even see him off at the station before he left for HMS Pembroke. Since then he had been sending the occasional letters to me via my sister in Scotland."

Geraldine looked down at her watch.

"I'm taking the Flying Scotsman and it leaves in 10 minutes, I ought to get going."

Again, I hoped she would leave a number or an address.

"Geraldine if I find Wayne ....."

"Please don't let Mrs Saunders know we have met," she pleaded. I don't want her to know we have spoken, or where I'm going. If you find

Wayne let him know I'm still thinking of him and miss him so much."

She got up to leave.

There was just one question I needed to ask before she left.

"What is it that frightens you about Mrs Saunders?" I enquired directly.

"Is it something you know about her, or her husband, or even Wayne?"

She stared at me accusingly.

"Why did you say that?" she darted back at me. "I've told you enough already."

She glanced at her watch again, nervously.

"I need to leave," she pleaded. I just wanted you to know about Wayne and that I wish him everything good in his life. You will tell him, won't you?"

"Geraldine," I tried to reassure her. "Trust me, I won't repeat any of our conversation with

Mrs Saunders but if it helps, please keep in touch and call me now and then."

I gave her my card.

"I am determined to find Wayne and I'll let him know I have met you and you are still thinking of him." I continued. "I'd like to pass him your address."

She withdrew uncertainly from the table. "Thank you Mr Moray. When I feel safe, I'll contact you. I hope you find Wayne and perhaps in time I'll call you and give you my address."

The Flying Scotsman was already in the station. I watched the small solitary figure walking stoically towards the train. She didn't look back once. Eventually she disappeared amongst an anonymous sea of people and the steam drifting across the platforms, reducing the crowds to ghostly floating shadows.

I was more than a little sad I couldn't get a forwarding address from her.

The nagging questions still stayed in my mind. What was the reason for her sudden departure from Mrs Saunders employ? What did she know that made her leave London to move right up to Scotland?

Without doubt Wayne was the key to all the questions but first I needed to call Mrs Saunders.

CHAPTER EIGHTEEN

I returned to the office still full of questions and found Gloria methodically working her way through the notebook.

I told Gloria I had met up with Geraldine and that the poor girl had just left Saunders employ. "She seemed quite scared," I said.

"There's something quite serious going on here but I can't seem to make it out," I said thinking back to my meeting with Geraldine. I wanted to just pick up the phone and ask Mrs Saunders why Geraldine had left. My gut feeling, however, told me that wouldn't be a smart move.

"Anything else going on in his notebook?" I asked

"Oh yes," Gloria replied, "Lots. Where do you want to start? There's an entry here where he seems to be back in the UK and visiting his

'Ma'. Listen: *Father died. Police. Ma at home.* And it's followed by the word '*muddy*'."

That made me sit up.

"There's a line after it saying, '*I'll make her pay for this*'."

"It's a long shot but it couldn't be 'murdered' could it?" I ventured.

"Oh my goodness. You could be right but it doesn't really make sense. You don't think Wayne murdered his Dad or she murdered her husband, do you?" Gloria asked in hushed tones.

I didn't answer that right away.

"I'll see if I can check out Harry's death certificate," I replied after a while. "But even Lester says he had a heart attack. Then again he wasn't there at the time, not even at the funeral. Also, Geraldine was off work that day." It struck me that to get to the truth, I would definitely have to find Wayne. Was he involved in something other than just pinching some

135

money? The clouds seemed to part slightly, making way for a clearer view of his mother's motivation to find Wayne. Was he a witness to murder? Had he escaped to the Navy and onward to America to blackmail her from there?

Too many questions and not enough answers

"You've gone a bit quiet," Gloria interrupted my thoughts.

Whether it was Wayne or his mother, that word 'murder' could well be correct and the missing piece of the puzzle.

"Perhaps Wayne murdered his father?" I said out loud, not believing it for a minute. "Or did his mother pay him to leave the country and set up in the States?"

What would she do that for, I asked myself?

Something told me I had got the wrong end of the stick.

"Gloria, can you check the local and national newspapers for around that time?" I continued after a while.

If it was a murder that would certainly have been publicised in the papers and there would have been a manhunt, surely?

"I'll get onto my old mate, Rob Barnsley, the veteran newshound on the *London Evening News* and see if I can meet up with him."

The phone rang and I lifted the receiver.

As if by telepathy it was Mrs Saunders.

"Any news?" she accused, cutting out the standard greetings.

"I'm still waiting for a response from the Naval base and started calling up contact numbers in the States, I fielded. So far nothing."

She sniffed a bit, obviously not impressed with my progress. Fortunately she didn't pursue it. It gave me a bit more breathing space.

At this point, I was wondering why Mrs Saunders had not followed up any of the phone numbers herself in his address book. She could have quite easily phoned instead of getting a complete stranger to make contact. Or perhaps she was just as much of a stranger as I was to Wayne and his friends?

On the other hand, having had the phone slammed down on me, and a total blank with some of the contacts, I deduced her direct contact would not be welcome. Once again, I was convinced something else mattered even more to Mrs Saunders than just tracking down the money. I was beginning to feel she wasn't just after Wayne for her money. There was something a little more sinister going on. I felt she was after her pound of flesh too.

I promised to get in touch with her as soon as I received anything concrete, then put the phone down.

Most of all, I didn't mention my meeting with Geraldine.

CHAPTER NINETEEN

The next day, I thought I would follow up my letter to the Naval base to appease Mrs Saunders. They weren't too keen to divulge anything. However, they did confirm that they had information on 1830 Squadron and an historical event which included the Corsairs. (*refer pp330-331) They were pleased to send this to me and I was more than happy to receive it. It would be good to expand on that notebook entry.

In the meantime, I had arranged to meet up with Rob Barnsley for a bit of lunch at the Chiltern Hall Restaurant in Baker Street. I hoped he may have found some good gossip on the Saunders.

"Wotcha cock, how ya doin'?" the loud voice from behind bellowed in my ear.

I turned round to see Rob, my old co-conspirator, grinning from ear to ear. He hadn't changed much, just slightly wider and less hair. We made our way into the beautiful restaurant with its fabulous décor and ordered the 'special' of fish and chips.

"Well? Did you find anything?" I asked after we had placed our order.

"You must be kiddin'," Rob joked. "*Man Dies of a Heart Attack* doesn't normally make the headlines. That said I rummaged in the archives to see what the papers had to say about Saunders and his Mrs and came up with a couple of gems."

Rather triumphantly Rob put two newspaper clippings on the table.

"These are the ones I found in the local papers," he smiled.

I looked at the articles, one of which read:

Harry Saunders, 25 Sidmouth Road, Willesden was summoned for using threats towards Perry Miles of Christchurch Avenue, Brondesbury.

"Funnily enough there was also a piece on Mrs Saunders," he laughed. "She's a right tartar and no mistake. Just listen to this."

This time Rob read the article out loud. *"A summons was made against Diana Saunders of 25 Sidmouth Road, Willesden, who was summoned for assaulting Mrs Muriel Miles."* He looked up at me. "They were quite a nasty pair really."

"I'd say they were made for each other," I nodded with a grin.

Rob pointed to the article and continued: "It was alleged that they used threats and that Diana Saunders struck Muriel Miles. Saunders denied that allegation, saying she never struck her. However, they ended up being bound over for 12 months for threatening behaviour and assault."

So Diana Saunders was not adverse to a bit of physical violence, I thought.

Rob stared at me ruefully. "Quite a feisty lady, your client."

"And here's another one. It describes Harry Saunders as having 'Pent-up Feelings' and being charged with assault." Rob read on: "Saunders was driving his car into his garage when he was approached by Ben Whitby. Saunders got out of his car and hit him."

Rob laughed.

"It's like a scene from Laurel & Hardy. He literally put his fist through the glass panel of Whitby's car and used bad language. No surprises there then."

I nodded in agreement.

"Whitby ended up with 3 loose teeth, swollen lips and cheek and was bleeding profusely from two cuts." Rob continued. "Mrs Saunders was also in the car and not being outdone got out and entered the fight too. What a pair!"

"Whitby and Saunders knew each other, you know, in fact it turned out that Whitby was employed by Saunders. He had threatened to report Saunders to the Old Bill for illegal street betting. Saunders ended up being put bang to rights and ordered to pay damages. Bit of a scoundrel that 'arry, I'd say."

I could see this was amusing Rob.

Then Rob showed me another article with a headline '*Kilburn Club Used for Betting.*'

I read the content: *A police raid on a Kilburn High Road Club where Harry Saunders, a bookmaker of Sidmouth Road, was arrested by Inspector Fuller and charged with using the premises for betting activities. He was fined and ordered to pay £6.6s costs and bound over for twelve months.*

"Serves him right," Rob said, and I nodded in agreement.

"Oh this one will make you laugh," Rob added, producing an article titled *Rounding Him Up*.

I read the article myself this time.

Harry Saunders was charged by his wife, with failing to pay £14.2s under an order of maintenance. It was stated that on a previous occasion he was allowed 21 days in which to pay the amount then due, and on the last day he paid. The magistrate ordered the payment of the £14 with the alternative of 2 months' imprisonment and refused to allow the accused any extra time.

Before I could ask how Diana Saunders managed to get him on maintenance, Rob intervened.

"Apparently, Harry Saunders had been married to Muriel Miles who was assaulted by Diana Saunders in that other article. Muriel is now living in Islington," he said. "Diana was his second wife. Now I followed this up and visited Muriel."

"Anything useful?" I asked.

"Well she wasn't too forthcoming, wanting to put the whole episode behind her," he said. "She was only prepared to confirm they were divorced on the grounds of adultery. Her passing shot at Harry, was that *they deserved each other.*"

"No love lost there then," I grinned.

The final article Rob showed me concerned a robbery: It read.... *On a further charge of breaking into a house in Sidmouth Road, and stealing a Persian lamb coat, necklace, brooch and suits of clothing worth £300 belonging to Mr & Mrs Harry Saunders.*

"Not short of a few bob by all accounts," Rob announced.

Diana Saunders must have been broken-hearted to have had her coat and jewellery nicked. I wondered how long it was before she got them replaced.

"What a couple," I declared. "Pretty devious and no strangers to the inside of the police cells, or the occasional fine."

The articles amused us throughout our lunch at the Chiltern Hall and gave me a perfect insight into the Saunders that they were capable of just about anything. But murder?

I thanked Rob for taking the time to dig up these little gems and finished off our meeting with a glass of wine and a promise to meet up again in the not too distant future. We said a cheerful farewell and both headed back to Baker Street station. It wasn't until I got to the States that I was going to rely on Rob again; this time to investigate something on Diana Saunders and an influential man in her life, other than her late husband.

*****

Back at the office, Gloria was working on the notebook for some hours whilst I skimmed through the address book.

"Hey, check this out, Gloria." I said at last. "Have you come across the name Margarita de los Dolores in the notebook?"

Gloria shook her head frowning. "No," she said, "but there is a Rita mentioned fairly often. Hang on... *Rita. Engagement party, book club.*"

We looked at each other.

It occurred to me that Rita or Margarita was probably one and the same person. She had to be one of the entries worth following up in his address book when I eventually left for the States.

Up to now there was no indication that Wayne was a full on homosexual. He had a fair entourage of female friends and admirers but there was his relationship with Guy in America. In my estimation he may well have been bisexual, or perhaps the females gave him the 'cover' needed to be what he wanted to be without detection.

Whatever his persuasion, it would make no difference to the investigation.

CHAPTER TWENTY

The following day the post arrived. It included a large brown envelope with an official looking stamp from the Royal Navy in Portsmouth.

The contents in the envelope verified Wayne's entry in his notebook. They read:

Corsairs of 1830 Squadron. routine flight. nine planes took off. One lost.

In addition, the envelope contained a copy of a letter from the Commanding Officer of the 1830 Squadron when aboard the aircraft carrier, HMS Illustrious. Wayne must have been witness to the lost pilots and planes and had typed out the letter sent to the Navy on behalf of the CO, whose nickname was "Ironside".

On reading the letter, it turned out it was "Ironside" of the 1830 Squadron who solved the mystery of the loss of pilots and planes. The

Commanding Officer had suffered the tragic loss of some of his young pilots on *HMS Illustrious* and was determined to do something about it. By all accounts "Ironside" had decided to go by his instincts to work out what was going wrong. He took up a plane and according to the letter made it back. Ultimately it was "Ironside" who saved the lives of many young pilots as the letter read:

To the Commanding Officer, British Squadrons, Washington.

"I have the honour to report my findings in the loss of four Corsair fighters; one on the 13th April, one on the 14th April and two on the 16th April 1943. I took my Corsair fighter over a trial run, exactly the same speeds and altitudes during the loss of these planes. When the plane flies at an altitude of 2,000 feet at an air speed of 300 miles per hour, the air mixture gives off poisonous fumes which seep into the cockpit. I had suspected such a happening, as none of the

pilots spoke to me over their R.D.F. before the crash, indicating they were unconscious, or unable to speak. I took up with me a special mask and container of oxygen and as soon as I noticed traces of carbon monoxide, I used my mask. I recommend that a special adjustment be made to the engine to eliminate this poisonous gas.

I have the honour to be,

Sir,

Your obedient Servant

COMMANDING OFFICER, 1830 Squadron

Sadly, this same brave CO went on another mission sometime later, but miscalculated his landing. He ended up in the sea, never to be recovered.

Wayne, it seemed, had witnessed this tragic event. (This is a factual event – refer pp330-331)

PART TWO – CITY OF ANGELS

CHAPTER TWENTY-ONE

Wayne received his discharge in black and white after one of the shortest careers ever in the Navy – six months.

Armed with his discharge papers, attaché case and duffle bag, Wayne struggled with the front gate; it was stuck as usual. He dropped his duffle bag and reached over the top of the gate to release the catch, as he had done numerous times before. As the gate squeaked open, the two-storey house seemed to bear down on him, opening up its arms in a threatening embrace. With some apprehension, Wayne picked up his duffle bag, threw it over his shoulder and in best Naval tradition, strutted down the front path, with a roll that would have put any sea-going sailor to shame.

The front door was open, airing out the house.

"Is that you, Wayne?" the familiar voice of his mother, came bellowing out from the upper part of the house.

"Yes," Wayne called back

"Don't come in the house with your dirty shoes on, I've just had the floors cleaned."

Out of habit he did as his mother told him, kicked off his shoes and dropped his kit.

He ran upstairs to show his mother his discharge papers.

Diana was sprawled out on a love-seat in her bedroom, face covered with cream and filing her fingernails.

"Aren't you hot in that horrible looking outfit you're wearing?" she snapped. "Why don't you put on your civvies? In fact, be a good boy and pass me those chocolates next to my bed before you go."

Once again, Wayne did as his mother ordered, then went to his bedroom to change his clothes. Before he had a chance to even open his case his mother called out again.

"Wayne?" she demanded from the next room, "Be a good boy and run across the street and see if you can get some cigarettes for your father. They may give you some if you tell them you're still in the Service. You don't have to tell them you're out."

She then continued her demands.

"Might as well stop in at the grocery store and see if you can get some eggs too," she continued filing her nails. "Your brother, Lester, has written to say he was trying to get home on leave this week, although it might not happen. You know how he goes for scrambled eggs and chicken livers. See if you can get some of those lovely little hard peppermints that I like so much."

Anything else Wayne wondered?

"I'll go just as soon as I've taken a bath," he said heading away from the constant demands. But he was stopped in his tracks.

"There's no fire on in the kitchen, no hot water so you'll have to wait until tomorrow," his mother's verbal agony continued. "If you put your uniform back on and go across the street right now, you'll just make it. Oh and your father wants you to pick him up at 5 o'clock this evening."

The orders were flowing quicker than on a Parade ground. It was one thing taking orders from his superiors but there was no rhyme or reason to take it from his mother.

"Haven't you gone yet, Wayne?" the demands continued on and on. "Get a move on, Wayne or the shops will close," she ordered. "Lay out for it and I'll pay you back later."

Wayne had been hoping for a loan till he received his cheque in a week or two.

"I just need a couple of bob until my cheque comes through," he pleaded.

She begrudgingly handed him ten shillings as if they were crown jewels.

"And don't forget to bring me back the change," she called out as he started to walk away. "Ask your father for pocket money when you see him tonight, he's got more than me." Wayne sighed and started for the sanctuary of the front door.

Outside the house was the same, the garden was the same, the front gate was the same – and worse luck, so was his mother.

CHAPTER TWENTY-TWO

So one step at a time.

I arrived at LA International and caught a Yellow Cab to an apartment I had booked off Sunset Boulevard. It turned out to be a perfect location in more ways than one. I later found I was nearer to Wayne than I could have imagined. I couldn't have chosen a better location even if I had tried.

The next day, slightly jetlagged, I strolled along Sunset Boulevard and found a restaurant to sit and watch the world go by. The interior was a picture of Formica, chrome, and brightly coloured comfortable booth seating. In contrast to the 'greasy spoon' in Kilburn High Road, it seemed you could almost eat your meal off the floor. In the centre of the main floor, a row of stools faced a circular dining counter that wrapped around two complete soda fountains. I thought it was a fascinating place. I also wondered if I could be sitting next to Wayne and not know it. After all, I only had a photograph to go by.

I got stuck into the notebook entries that Gloria had now deciphered and typed out. It seemed customary to have a waffle and coffee and so I decided to indulge even though it was still breakfast time according to my body clock. Do as the 'Romans' do I told myself.

A waitress came over and I ordered a massive waffle with a drizzle of maple syrup plus my morning dose of caffeine in the shape of a strong cup of coffee. And there I sat in the strong Californian sunshine with my waffle and coffee watching the beautiful bodies stroll by. I had time after all and I could get used to this way of life I told myself.

I realised very quickly that to get around the city I would either have to grab a cab each time or, better still, I decided to hire a car so I could move around the place easily. And what a choice of cars. I ended up with a Cadillac that made my Ford Anglia 'rust bucket' seem like something out of toy town. The Cadillac bounced on the suspension and I felt as though I was sitting on a trampoline. After a short time I got used to the left hand drive and the luxury of an automatic, no gearstick. I just had to remember to drive on the right hand side of the road.

I used that first day to get used to my surroundings, try and acclimatise and enjoy the mega-sized portions of food which appeared to be the norm.

*****

When I woke up the following morning, I phoned through to Diana Saunders to let her know I had arrived but there was no answer.

I looked out my apartment window and it was just like a London fog, only here it was 'smog'. Same air pollution just a different name. The visibility was so reduced I decided to stay in the apartment and work through the address book.

Many of the numbers I tried gave an 'unobtainable' signal; a couple of others answered but were reluctant to take it any further and cut short any conversation over the phone. They just confirmed they knew Wayne but were not prepared to talk to me without his knowledge. I asked one or two of them if they would pass my details onto Wayne. They all declined.

Then I came across the name, Margarita de los Dolores. This could very well be the "Rita" that Gloria had identified and translated in the notebook with the words *engagement* and *book the club*. I dialled the number.

Magarita wasn't in but it turned out she owned the nightclub, *Ciro*'s, just on a corner of

Sunset Boulevard, which was practically opposite my apartment. It was good to finally have a contact that might be able to reach Wayne. At least Margarita definitely existed and I was curious about the "engagement". I had assumed by this time that Wayne's engagement to Margarita was a curved ball. I mean what with his past lover, Guy, and my own research, it left me little doubt that Wayne was homosexual.

It turned out that *Ciro*'s was a night club that attracted up and coming starlets and randy producers from the Hollywood set. In many ways it was an extension of the casting couch. I could see how Wayne was attracted to the club and ultimately to Margarita. The engagement may well have been Wayne's introduction to the Hollywood scene but I was curious why it didn't come to anything. Much more important, I hoped Margarita was still in contact with Wayne.

I persevered and rang Margarita a number of times but got no answer. Busy lady I told myself.   It seemed that the only way I was going to reach her was to go in person to the nightclub.   It was actually within walking distance of my apartment but I did what everyone in LA seemed to do and that was to drive to the Club. I was looking forward, not only to meeting Margarita, but also visiting the hottest spot on "The Strip" – *Ciro*'s.

I decided to make a night of it. It would be the only way to get a chance to speak to Margarita and any celebrities strutting their stuff there would be a bonus.

CHAPTER TWENTY-THREE

Magarita de los Dolores.   Wow!   She was the Rita in Wayne's address book.   Now how do I describe this absolutely drop dead gorgeous woman?   She was sort of a cross between Ava Gardner and Rita Hayworth with similar smouldering Latino looks.   All in all, it made it very hard for me to concentrate when I was at last introduced to her.

I had arrived about an hour before the place opened in the hope she would make time to speak to me.

"I'm sorry to turn up out of the blue but it was really urgent that I speak to you," I announced.

Margarita seemed somewhat taken aback by my English accent but obliged me by taking the time to talk.

"You've come a long way to find Wayne," she said suspiciously. "Come into the backroom where we can speak more privately."

I took up the invitation and followed the mesmerising swivel of her hips to the back room.

"Now, tell me again why you want to contact Wayne?" she asked directly in a smooth voice that matched the rest of her body and almost knocked me to the floor.

"It's a delicate matter," I replied. "Is there any possibility I could speak to Wayne even over the phone?"

Margarita looked directly at me, seeming to be momentarily furious. "Who put you up to this?"

"His mother." I confessed without hesitation. I suddenly felt I had been cornered as her eyes widened in response.

"Are you kiddin'?" she sighed, shaking her long luxurious hair.

I couldn't help but pause in shock at her directness.

"What does she want of him after all this time?" she uttered in a low enquiring tone.

"Some money he owed her, by all accounts," I feebly replied.

"And you believed that crock of shit?" she shot back at me with her large brown eyes blazing.

"Don't shoot the messenger," I gallantly replied raising my hands in surrender.

I needed to put my cards on the table, and fast.

"OK I was hired by Mrs Saunders to find her son," I confessed. "But I do feel morally bound to hear Wayne's side of the story."

"I'm not sure Wayne wants to even be reminded his mother is alive!" was her unflinching retort. "Please don't tell me she's here, that would just kill him."

I tried to reassure her that there was no need for Diana to come to Los Angeles. After all she was paying me to find Wayne and report back.

This seemed to placate Rita a bit but I could tell she was still wary of my intentions.

"I'll call him and let him make up his mind if he wants to meet you," she said after a while. As far as I was concerned this was a breakthrough. I almost sighed out loud.

Rita got up. I offered her a card from the apartment that I was renting. I felt it was a good moment to ask her to let Wayne know that I had met with Geraldine and would she please pass on her regards to him. I hoped that this would show that I had heard from an ally and it might entice Wayne to call me.

"Have a drink on the house," Rita said as she moved towards the main club, thereby indicating the abrupt end of our meeting. She had work to do and celebrities to *schmooze*.

I stayed and had a drink watching Gary Cooper and Frank Sinatra arrive with ladies in tow. My jet lag wasn't going to allow me to keep awake much longer and besides my expenses didn't stretch to nightclub entertainment. I decided to leave.

I looked around for Rita to say goodbye but she was busy rubbing shoulders with the rich and famous. I just hoped she had enough faith in me to contact Wayne. I jumped into my bouncy Cadillac and within minutes was back in my apartment and crashed out till the morning.

*****

I was just sipping my first coffee of the morning when the phone rang.

"Hi, this is Wayne Saunders," a strong voice with a Californian accent said. "Rita asked me to call you."

I nearly fell off my chair. The last thing I expected was a call from the man himself so shortly after the meeting with Rita, if at all.

I gathered my wits and answered.

"Hi, this is Charlie Moray speaking. I'm really grateful you've called."

There was a slight pause.

"Rita tells me this is something to do with my mother," he added finally.

"Yes, she is behind my search for you." I decided a direct approach was best.

"What does she want?" he responded bitterly. "Has she sent you for her pound of flesh?"

This was no longer going well I thought.

"I'm sorry for the intrusion into your life and I know it's a big ask," I said hoping to appeal to his emotional side. "However, is there any chance we could meet up? It would be easier to do this face to face. Then, if what I have to say is not what you want to hear, I'll leave and tell your mother nothing."

Once more there was an awkward silence.

"You've come a long way just to return empty-handed." Wayne sighed sympathetically. "I imagine she's paying you very well."

"Not as much as you may imagine," I replied with equal lightness in my voice. "I'd like you to know that I've met up with your friend, Guy. He's now living in Cornwall. He was very keen to let you know there were no hard feelings in any way and would even like to link up again."

I thought I detected a slight intake of breath.

"I'll think about that one," Wayne cautiously replied.

There was a further short pause during which time it must have dawned on him that I must have Guy's and Rita's numbers from somewhere.

"How did you know about Guy and Rita?" he enquired.

"Your mother had your address book which she passed to me," I replied.

"I thought I might have lost it but on the other hand, I did leave in rather a hurry," he now recalled. "I'm surprised my mother didn't go through it to call up friends and spread more lies about me."

"I think she may have tried," I said knowingly. "I do have the notebook with me in Los Angeles."

"Now, THAT I did miss," his tone seemed to lighten.

"I would be more than happy to return it to its rightful owner, in person if we could meet up," I suggested expectantly.

"I'd love to have it back. I assume you've got the address book as well?"

"I have," I said immediately.

I felt the atmosphere was changing and he was coming round to the idea of meeting up, even if it was just to return his address book and notebook. Gloria had finished translating it and typed it all out neatly, so I had a copy with me as well.

"OK, tomorrow at 12 noon," he said decisively. "Let's meet at Beverley Hills Hotel, you can't miss it. It's totally pink." I heard his laughter at the other end of the line.

"I'll get in touch with Rita," he added. "I'd like her to come along, so she'll pick you up on the way."

He asked me for my address and laughed again. I didn't get that one until we met the next day.

CHAPTER TWENTY-FOUR

Rita picked me up and we arrived at the Beverley Hills Hotel on the dot of 12, high noon without the horses and cowboy hats! The hotel was as Wayne had described, totally pink, and known as "The Pink Palace". The exterior in pink could not be missed.   We headed for the Polo Lounge.

The man I had seen in the photographs was tall, good looking and made for American movies. He was now walking towards me. We shook hands and I felt an immediate connection. Perhaps it was because I was English and he was born in England. At least that may have had something to do with it. The fact that I had met with his brother, Lester, had made me feel much more relaxed too.

We found a comfortable corner and sat down.   A waiter came over and we ordered some drinks. I broke the ice by asking Wayne why he had laughed when I gave him my address at the apartment on Sunset Boulevard.

"I live off Sunset, up a steep hill, Miller Drive, almost opposite your apartment," he said and then paused. "I've got nothing to hide and you can tell her I don't owe her anything!" he blurted after a while. "In fact, she owes me more than she could ever repay me. If you want the full story, it may take some time."

I felt it was like being in the presence of a volcano. One minute he really erupted, then just as quickly relaxed as our drinks arrived and were served. Wayne noticeably dropped his American accent and slipped comfortably back into the London vernacular of his birth.

Wayne nodded towards Rita who up to now had remained silently listening to the exchange with growing uneasiness.

"I don't think I'm needed here and I've got some business to attend to," she quietly said. "I'll come back in about an hour, if that's OK?"

Wayne turned to me and I nodded in acceptance.

Wayne got up to air kiss Rita, who then did the most mesmerising walk out of the lounge.

"What an absolutely stunning woman," I couldn't resist remarking as we watched her walk away. "Were you an item back in the day?"

I decided to be blunt and Wayne didn't hesitate in his reply.

"Yes, in fact, we were engaged at one time but Rita broke it off." He looked down in seemingly genuine sorrow. "Circumstances," he said almost in a whisper.

"But we have remained good friends ever since." His tone lightened. "You know the old saying: *All the nice girls love a sailor* but does a nice sailor necessarily love a girl?"

Wayne left that remark open and laughed it off. I didn't know him well enough to assume anything. It was a foregone conclusion that Wayne was homosexual but we were in sensitive times and to marry was a safe way out.

There was a further pause while Wayne and I settled back into the sumptuous surroundings.

"As for my mother," Wayne continued. "It's impossible to describe the rift between us. It would take more than an hour to tell the whole story. I have to admit I am concerned about her sudden push to track me down. It's been some years since she's even tried to contact me."

"She told me that you owed her a considerable sum of money." I offered the only reason I had.

"It isn't that," he snapped with real conviction. "I'm not even sure I can tell you what it's all about without getting *her* locked up."

My eyebrows must have hit the top of my hairline.

"I'll have to think about it," Wayne said thoughtfully, then switched the subject.

"Rita mentioned that you had met Geraldine," he enquired after a while. "What's Geraldine doing now?"

"Geraldine's alright," I assured him, "but she's left the employ of your mother. I met her just before she was getting on a train to stay with her sister in Scotland. She is desperate to hear from you and wanted me to let you know that she misses you and to please write."

"I have her sister's address, but haven't written to her in a while," Wayne sounded regretful.

"Perhaps you could assure her all is well," I offered. "She was understandably anxious to say too much, even though she had met up with me before. In fact, she was somewhat hesitant to trust me entirely. I couldn't blame her really.

Instead, she had promised to call me some time, in the hope I'd have some news on you. I'd like to tell her that I've seen you and that you're OK."

"I'll think about it," he replied seeming less convinced now.

It was our first meeting, and I know I shouldn't have expected too much. Instead, I resorted to chatting about his life here in Los Angeles.

This turned out to be the first of a few meetings, by which time I wasn't sure whose side I was on.

The acrimony between Wayne and his mother was obvious but it was evident that his move to Los Angeles had cut him off from any of the family, and in particular his brother, Lester. If she was after money, it was obvious Wayne felt she could whistle for it. In fact, he said he could get her locked up – what was that all about?

I was ending up with more questions than answers

CHAPTER TWENTY-FIVE

Reading the notebook, I had discovered that Wayne had been employed at Paramount Pictures, Century City when he first arrived in Tinsel Town. Wayne started as an extra in Cecil B DeMille's remake of *The Ten Commandments*. He then did some more work out there but moved on to 20th Century Studios, also located in Century City where he got caught up in the celebrity that is Marilyn Monroe.

I thought I could "kill two birds with one stone" and visit both studios.

I had heard nothing from either 20th Century Fox or Paramount both of whom I had written to before I left the UK. I decided to call in person and made an appointment to see the Personnel officers at the studios.

My day's mission established, I got behind the wheel of my trusty Cadillac and drove over to Melrose Avenue and Paramount studios. It wasn't far. Indeed, if I was home I would have walked it! On arrival, I entered through the famous archway and headed for the parking bay. It certainly was a fascinating place. The uniformed guard directed me past various backlots and Stage 18 or the "Cecil B. DeMille Stage" which was huge. Outside the converted streets and lots were buzzing with rehearsals going on. I saw Charlton Heston and Yul Brynner walk by as I strolled towards the administration block.

"Do come in," a welcoming voice called me into the office.

Her name was Sheila Dorset, the Personnel Officer who had agreed to see me. It was going to be a gamble whether or not she would be forthcoming with details on Wayne. As I had now met Wayne, I didn't need an address, just some background information.

Sheila was happy to give me a list of the 'movies' Wayne had featured in as an extra culminating in his recent scenes in *The Ten Commandments*. Wayne's physique was his golden ticket into the movie industry. Later Wayne was given roles as an extra in the film itself. He then moved on to Twentieth Century Studios. I thanked Sheila and left to drive onwards to 20th Century Lot.

Nothing prepared me for the shock I encountered as I pulled in through the Studio entrance. I couldn't believe my eyes and it caught me up sharp. There was Diana Saunders getting out of a car accompanied by a tall chap, smartly dressed and definitely more than a friend. He was obviously not one of the staff. She was far too chummy with him for that. No wonder I wasn't getting answers to my calls or telegram.

Diana was already here!

I had noticed those legs when she entered my offices all those months ago but this time they were being uncurled from a smart Cadillac.

The bonnet of the car made me look twice. It was encrusted with Rhinestones. Where on earth did she get all this money from? I then looked over to see who her companion was. The man in the driving seat looked familiar but he had his back to me. I felt I should linger a little, as I was counting on that known fact that if you're not expecting to see someone, you don't always see them.

I hoped Diana Saunders would come up against the same brick wall as I did, in trying to get Wayne's address but I really couldn't count on that now that I knew she was ahead of me.

This put a whole new perspective on things.

I decided to make myself scarce. I didn't want to meet up with her but was really curious as to why she hadn't told me she was here. I had my suspicions that the man she was with, strolling arm in arm, was the one and only Inspector Fuller.

The sight of Diana Saunders really bothered me. I couldn't understand what she was up to, after all, she was paying me to find Wayne. There had to be some desperation in her turning up without letting me know.

I headed back to my apartment

*****

The phone rang at midnight, dragging me from a deep sleep.

"Have you found anything yet?" A female voice accused.

There was no mistaking that sharp tone. Diana Saunders was pretending to call from London.

"Do you know what time it is?" I responded sleepily playing for time.

"I'm not paying you to sleep," was her fast retort.

I had to get my wits together as I didn't want to even hint that I had met Wayne.

"I'm working through the contacts in the address book, but so far I've come up against a brick wall," I lied.

The palpable silence on the line suggested she was unconvinced.

"Many of the people have either moved, died or even put the phone down on me," I continued. "To tell the truth it's a bit disconcerting to find so many people don't want to talk, or just getting the phone slammed down."

"That just shows you what sort of people he moved around with," she replied without a second thought.

Yes I reflected. But the phone was usually slammed down only when I mentioned her name.

"I'm hoping to get to the studios tomorrow," I said playing for time. "If I hear anything, I'll call you back."

"No don't bother," she rasped rudely. "I'm planning to go away for a week or so. I'll call you when I have a moment."

Without more ado she slammed the phone down.

"Thank you and goodbye!" I said to the wall.

It suddenly struck me she may have been following me all the time. I had to get a grip. I was starting to have paranoid thoughts. It was certainly becoming rather sinister, like a game of cat and mouse. The problem was I had to work out which one of us was the cat and who was the mouse.

I also had to decide whether to share the news with Wayne that his mother was, indeed, in town and almost certainly looking for him.

CHAPTER TWENTY-SIX

Seeing Diana Saunders surreptitious trip to the studios with Inspector Fuller in tow, I resolved I needed to see Wayne again fast. Providence then intervened when he phoned me the morning after his mother's call, inviting me to his home later that day.

Wayne came and picked me up. His home was, as he said, quite literally down the road from where I was staying. It was a modest house compared to the surrounding properties but tastefully decorated nonetheless.

"I haven't always lived here," Wayne informed me. "I used to have an apartment on Valencia Street in San Francisco when I first moved to the States."

"It's a nice place," I commented and meant it. The house had two bedrooms and a bathroom and overlooked an amazing city view.

"Yes, I've been lucky," he replied. "My film work's allowed me to purchase exactly the kind of property I always wanted. Come downstairs and let me show you."

I followed Wayne downstairs to a living room dominated by a huge fireplace. On the far side facing the fireplace was the kitchen.

"Fashion dictated I had to get an Aga oven," he laughed. "I don't know why because I only use it for heating the place in the winter and boiling eggs in the summer."

The grand tour continued. Wayne was very clearly proud of his house. It had an additional back room which housed the bar and there was also the deck.

Unlike the neighbour's deck which was built solidly of concrete and marble, however, Wayne's was built on wooden stilts.

It even felt it had an unnerving slant downwards as we stepped onto the wooden boards.

Wayne noticed my slight anxiety not only at the height but the thought that the wood might give way at any moment.

"Don't worry," he smiled. "I've lived here for years and it's still standing. That said I have thought of putting a hazard tape round. You know how quick they are to sue round here!"

Wayne laughed with a raise of an eyebrow.

None of this banter really relieved my anxiety at all as I tentatively looked down, trying not to lean against what looked like a weak wooden fencing.

The Panoramic views of the Hollywood Hills that stretched right over to the glistening city lights was absolutely breathtaking. Wayne said that Vincent Price lived nearby and through the slight smog, he pointed out across the valley-like drop to where Liberace's impressive house stood. It seemed that Wayne had visited the flamboyant performer on several occasions and was on good terms with him. Liberace delighted in showing off his home and the chandeliers. His jewellery was eye-watering, and included an appropriate "piano-shaped" ring.

"I got to see the house, even the closets!" Wayne cheerfully boasted. "And you know what Liberace said? 'Ah, you're a 'girl' after my own heart!'"

Wayne laughed and went on to describe the closets with mirrored doors and different coloured lighting inside containing the carefully colour co-ordinated clothes hanging there for all to see.

"To keep the money rolling in he threw open his house to the public for tours at $7.50 also showing off his nine sequined cars parked in his garage," Wayne said. "The neighbours complained about the lines and lines of long black limos carrying his *blue rinse* fans, so they took him to court. The tours were stopped."

Wayne chuckled at this amusing anecdote.

"Would you like some coffee?" he offered, and after a while we sat out on the slanting deck.

In all the time we spoke, he never really mentioned his mother, as if she didn't exist.

This caused me some concern as part of me felt I should warn him that his mother was in town and possibly up to no good.

"Did you get a chance to see Lester and Hannah?" Wayne asked at last.

"Yes," I replied, "I was really fortunate to meet up with them and their lovely children, even though it was just the once."

Wayne smiled, and seemed genuinely touched with emotion.

"I'm really pleased to hear that," he said with real feeling. "My brother and I haven't been in touch for years. I missed Lester at Dad's funeral but it was good to see Hannah there. She was lovely, in every way. "I only met her a couple of times when I went to the UK but it was good to see Lester with his brood!"

Wayne was beginning to reminisce now and I was starting to see a side of him I wasn't aware of before.

"Nice memories," he continued. "I was already working out so I was pretty fit. His kids liked swinging on my biceps and telling me I was stronger than their Dad!"

"Did you know that Hannah was having a hard time with your mother?" I questioned.

Wayne's smile at the fond memories of his brother and family suddenly faded.

"Lester needed to move into Ma's house while he was building up his business and while they lived under her roof, I'm convinced she spread her poison through his marriage." Wayne said bitterly. "My brother will pay the price for standing by our mother; he'll end up losing his wife and kids."

This came as a shock to me as there was no indication in my meeting with Lester and his wife that their relationship was in jeopardy. It wasn't evident on my visit that Hannah was already looking for a divorce and planning to leave with the children. In time Lester would come home to an empty house and divorce papers. Hannah ending up packing, collecting the children from school and leaving him.

Clearly there was a void between the brothers. Frankly they were like chalk and cheese, yet I could still detect there was this sibling bond which could not be erased.

"Hannah wanted me to warn you that your mother was looking for you," I added poised to broach the subject that Diana Saunders was already in town.

"She knew," was all Wayne said.

"Knew what?" I asked, perhaps too rapidly.

"That's for another time," Wayne smiled thinly without giving anything away.

He changed the subject.

"Ma managed to pocket away Dad's winnings before he gambled them away. That's how she was able to afford to buy food, hide away some jewellery and even have a maid, which was Geraldine. By the way, did Geraldine leave my mother's employ voluntarily?" he added with some concern.

There was no mistaking the anxiety in Wayne's voice.

"When I saw Geraldine at the station, she was relieved to have left and was looking forward to moving in with her sister," I added. "She gave in her notice, but I can't help feeling she was really scared of any repercussions your mother might have in line for her. Sorry, but I couldn't get to the bottom of it."

"She was more than a maid to me," Wayne said with great tenderness. "She was my rock, more like an older sister to me. She gave me the confidence to join the Navy. But most important of all, I'm not sure I would still be around if it wasn't for her."

"What do you mean," I ventured.

"I felt suicidal at times but she was always there for me, saving me from myself," he continued with great feeling. "I'll write a letter to her for you to take back." Wayne seeming both relieved and reassured that Geraldine had escaped from his mother's evil clutches.

"That will be great, as she so wanted you to know she was thinking of you." I said with all sincerity. "I'll be more than happy to take a letter back."

These were clearly intimate matters where Wayne was concerned and I felt it was a statement of trust that he confided in me in this way.

"Did you know Geraldine came and bailed me out of the Police Station when I was arrested for wearing my Naval uniform when I wasn't on duty?" Wayne finally said.

"Geraldine did mention this when we last met." I informed Wayne. "She was still upset about the whole incident."

"I just couldn't return home and Geraldine said I could stay at her place." Wayne continued. "The Hearing was set at the Probationary Court. We arrived early and went to a nearby café."

Suddenly Wayne's tone and expression changed.

"As we sat down, we saw my folks across the road," Wayne remembered. "I couldn't understand what they were doing there and worse luck they spotted us and came over."

"What happened," I ventured.

"'You good for nothing tramp' was my mother's first words to Geraldine," Wayne explained. "She was so shocked and embarrassed at Ma's outburst and on top of that, my father shouted at me to let go of her arm and called me a little 'toe rag'. It was then, out of the blue, Inspector Fuller arrived on the scene".

Wayne appeared to be vividly recollecting the whole scene.

"He was always around," Wayne continued bitterly. "He seemed to know my Dad well and my Ma even better, if you know what I mean."

There was no mistaking the sarcasm in Wayne's words. After a pause he resumed speaking almost like a confessional.

"I didn't trust him." Wayne added with vitriolic emphasis.

Inspector Fuller, I thought to myself, *I didn't trust him either.*

"What happened next?" I asked.

"The Probationary Officer arrived and I had to leave Geraldine and go with my parents and Inspector Fuller," Wayne continued.

This was my opportunity to delve deeper.

"This Inspector Fuller seems to have a strong connection with the family," I ventured. "He always seems to pop up when least expected."

"Like I said, I didn't trust him," Wayne emphasised and continued his story back at the court. "I still remember my day in court with Judge Whitcombe presiding. Geraldine was there smiling reassuringly at me in the Court Room as I took my place in the witness box and heard them announcing: first case, The Crown versus Wayne Saunders. The Judge picked up the complaint and studied it and then proceeded to question me."

"Did you have anyone representing you?" I asked.

"I went through the Probationary Officer and told the court there was nothing really to tell," Wayne frankly and truthfully responded. I was discharged from the service five or six weeks back and was going out the house and just decided to wear my uniform. I didn't realise I was doing anything wrong."

"What was the outcome?" I enquired.

"I was given a good talking to about how wonderful my parents were and how much I should appreciate them. I was then told to make it up with them, or I'd get a little stretch in prison. I knew my mother would prefer I took the latter choice to teach me a lesson."

"So those were your options," I said, "Make it up with your parents and go back home, or jail? Not much choice there."

"My mind was made up for me," Wayne concluded. Judge Whitcombe studied the contents of the hearing and in a few moments announced that I was exonerated of all charges placed before him. It was quite a relief until he declared it was on condition that I lived at home until I was ordered back to the Navy in the Writer Branch."

"That was that then," I suggested.

Wayne smiled without mirth.

"You'd think so," he said. "But in some ways I would have rather stayed in the cells than go home."

Now came the bit that I was dreading. The more I heard about Diana Saunders, the more I felt that I needed to warn Wayne that his mother was in town with a certain Inspector Fuller in tow.

I braced myself before delivering the blow.

"Wayne, I work for your mother and I'm supposed to respect client confidentiality," I began. "That said, all bets are off when a client isn't straight with me and doesn't keep me in the picture. Wayne, I saw your mother in Los Angeles yesterday at the studio and she had someone with her who I can only assume is Inspector Fuller."

Wayne looked at me in a short but shocked silence.

"I see," he said slowly, "In that case we need to <u>really</u> talk.   You had better stay for lunch."

CHAPTER TWENTY-SEVEN

"Well sir, a red annulus is incendiary and a brown annulus is armour piercing."

"Right, so why did you give me the armour piercing then?"

*****

Wayne seemed to calm down as he prepared what I can only describe as a Hollywood lunch. While initially shocked at the bombshell that his mother was in LA looking for him, he also seemed to accept the fact that she would eventually catch up with him and forewarned was forearmed. He began to reminisce as to the number of times his mother's jewellery ended up in the pawn shop and she had to eventually retrieve it.

"It was really quite humiliating," he shamefully confided. "She'd get that irritated with Dad she would go to the point of leaving his bed and I would find her in mine. It was a most uncomfortable relationship all round."

A far from natural situation I thought.

"At least you had your brother," I coaxed to lighten the mood.

"Yes, but you know how siblings are?" Wayne said with a late sorrow. "He was clearly Ma's favourite and I felt inferior to him and then grew to resent him for all the wrong reasons. I remember we even got into a fight about it."

"A fight?" I ventured.

"Yes," Wayne continued, as he shared out the portions of food. "She broke up the fight then took me by the scruff of my neck and forced me to kneel over the bathtub with blood dripping from my mouth down onto the white porcelain of the tub. I then had to scrape the congealed blood from the bathtub. And to top it all, she then took all my wages that week. I hated everything about living in that house."

"So getting your call up papers was a bit of relief," I suggested.

"Lester got his first," Wayne said. "He went off and joined the RAF. But then he failed his pilot's test."

"Why was that?" I said tucking into the meal.

"They discovered he was colour-blind, a condition passed on through my mother," he explained.

"Does that mean you're colour blind too?" I asked.

"Oh yes, we discovered that when I got caught out dismantling ammunition." Wayne said. "I remember the Instructor telling me that breaking down a 35mm gun wasn't all meat and potatoes. We then had to put it back together again and make sure it worked as someone's life would depend on our accuracy one day. He went on to explain that at the bottom of these bullets or shells, we have different colour annulus, red for incendiary ... and brown for amour piercing. This was the beginning of my colour-blind revelation."

"What did he make you do?" I asked.

"He instructed us to break them down to see what makes them tick, literally." Wayne grinned awkwardly. "He taught us what guns to use them in and whether or not they could be used together and learn all about them."

So far, so good, I thought.

"Then the instructor told us to pass round an incendiary shell," Wayne continued. "I finished inspecting both specimens and threw one back to him. I so remember him checking it and then hesitating before he shouted that he wanted the incendiary shell, not the armour piercing."

"Crickey, that doesn't sound too good!" I replied.

"I insisted I had given him the correct incendiary but things just got worse," Wayne continued remembering the incident. "The Instructor already had realised I was colour blind and was flabbergasted that I had got this far without it being detected."

"I've never known anyone who was colour-blind, that must have made things really awkward for you," I said concerned.

"I was put on report and sent to Portsmouth and treated as though I had some kind of affliction. It was so embarrassing," Wayne recalled. "They pulled out a bag with different coloured pieces of wool, each tied in a knot. All the colours started to look alike. I was really in a state and just made up any colour even though I knew everything depended on my answers. That's how I ended up as a Writer, rather than a pilot."

We finished the meal and Wayne smiled as if in conclusion.

"Just do me one favour," he said after a while. "The next time you come back please bring my address and notebook, they mean a great deal to me."

I assured him I would and left his house relieved both that I had warned him of his mother's impromptu arrival in Tinsel Town, and also that he had appeared to have taken the news relatively well.

I could only guess what was really going on and what the possible outcome of this might be.

CHAPTER TWENTY-EIGHT

The ambulance and the Police were outside the house in Sidmouth Road. The plain-clothed policeman was at the top of the stairs consoling Diana Saunders. She seemed very comfortable in his arms. It was Geraldine's day off but she was never off on a Monday.

*****

More and more I had become convinced that it was time to pursue my suspicions about this Inspector Fuller. My best bet was to once more contact my news hound pal, Rob Barnsley, to see what more he could tell me about this character.

"Before I start, are you sitting comfortably?" Rob's familiar voice almost sang down the phone line.

"As always," I said already smiling to myself.

"OK then, I'll begin."

I imagined Rob with a smug look on his face.

"For a start your Inspector Fuller keeps interesting company," Rob said. "He was stationed at Willesden and had quite a connection to the Saunders family but that's only the half of it."

"I see," I nodded. "You'd better dish the dirt then."

"For one thing Fuller was as bent as a nine bob note," Rob said getting into his stride.

"I sort of guessed that one," I laughed.

"Fuller knew Diana and Harry well," Rob continued. "He was often seen taking time out to visit Diana when her husband was at work. The rumour was that she was in his company on a regular basis."

Now we're getting somewhere, I thought.

"And you're gonna love this," Rob paused for effect and I waited expectantly for the punchline.

"Who do you think was part of the company Inspector Fuller kept after hours?" Rob was goading me on. "Go on, take a guess."

Rob was really dragging out the agony.

"No idea," I responded lightly. "But I'm sure this is going to be a headliner. I feel an exposé coming on."

"One of his drinking pals was the very same coroner, who 'looked after' Harry Saunders when he died," Rob concluded with obvious pride.

Well I wasn't expecting that one.

"I can check Harry's death certificate for any tell-tale signature," Rob offered.

"You're on," I replied eagerly.

CHAPTER TWENTY-NINE

The following morning I arrived at Miller Drive to hand back the notebook and address book to its rightful owner.

Once more Wayne and I settled down with a cup of coffee to continue our chat.

It seemed a good time to mention my background as a police officer and how I ultimately became a Private Investigator. I explained to Wayne that about midway through my career as a PI I met Harry Saunders. I told him I had first met his father, albeit briefly, when he came to my offices trying to get off a charge for betting out of hours. This anecdote really amused Wayne and it opened up a light-hearted conversation about his Dad.

"My Dad entertained both the wealthy and notorious gambling set of London and I found it mildly entertaining during the time I worked with him before joining the Navy," Wayne said reminiscing at the times spent with his father. "The time he went to see you to get him out of police clutches was when he slipped a large wad of notes under my book when I was working with him at the club and it got raided."

An expression of realisation came over Wayne's face.

"Come to think of it Inspector Fuller was the arresting officer then," he remarked.

I had never met Inspector Fuller at the time but everything was now falling into place and I nodded knowingly. It was a lightbulb moment for both of us.

"The war changed things for my Dad as he wasn't eligible for military service," Wayne continued. "Instead of studying Racing forms, he was found on the top of strange buildings, half asleep scanning the skies for enemy raiders. He hated it. That said, he wasn't an Air Raid Precautions Warden for long. As you know, the force of the German bombing raiders started to diminish gradually as the RAF Spitfires brought down more and more of the enemy raiders."

Wayne smirked.

"Ma, with just a thought for her own safety, had been evacuated to Surrey because she was really frightened of the raids," he said. "It was probably the only thing that did frighten her and Surrey was hardly her style. She returned as soon as she could because she had missed the luxury of her home, her maid, Geraldine, and to some extent the thrill of Dad's dodgy associations."

I was glad Wayne had mentioned Geraldine, she had been on my mind a while now.

"How did Geraldine get on with your mother at that time? I asked. "When I met her she seemed quite scared of your mother."

"She probably was," Wayne proclaimed with some conviction. "Everyone was frightened of Ma. I never brought friends home 'cos most of the time she didn't approve. It's true to say that Geraldine was my sanity!"

Wayne hesitated as if to sidestep the 'fear' issue.

"Let's just say that Geraldine didn't like being alone in the house with Ma when I was away," he added earnestly. "After Dad died things changed for Geraldine. Prior to his death, Dad was quite ill and Ma managed to get him certified and sent to Shenley – a Victorian place located in extensive grounds. It was very gothic and very eerie."

"Your mother mentioned this," I admitted.

"I bet she did," Wayne replied indignantly.

"Dad was a voluntary patient and wasn't that crazy 'cos he managed to have enough sense to get out of there."

Wayne hesitated then asked cautiously: "Did she mention that he died of a heart attack?"

"Yes," I nodded. "She told me that practically on our first meeting."

"He was hardly cold in his grave when she was already rummaging through his bureau," Wayne recalled. "That was where he kept his legal papers. I was standing in the doorway to his study and saw her wave a legal looking document in her hand, like it was Excalibur."

Wayne waved his hand in the air as if he'd just won the marathon.

"Got it!" she cried out triumphantly not realising I was standing behind her." Wayne said.

"So she didn't see you?" I asked.

"Only when it was too late," Wayne replied. "She had such a furtive look on her face when she turned to find me standing just a few feet away."

"What was the document? Your Dad's life insurance?" I guessed.

"Yes, spot on," Wayne quipped. "She had even managed to get him to update it very recently; you can check the date for what I think is quite a coincidence. She didn't take long to go through the motions and claim the proceeds."

I knew I could be skating on thin ice here. If I pushed too hard, there was always the danger that Wayne would clam up and cease talking to me at all. But there was an all-pervading question like the elephant in the room that I needed to address.

"From what you said earlier, Wayne, you seemed to imply that there was some question around the circumstances of your father's heart attack."

"Yes, well, any involvement Ma had in my father's death was confirmed by her actions." He almost spat the words out. "Let's say she was up to her neck in bathwater."

I was almost shocked by the vehemence of his response.

"What do you mean, *her involvement*?" I continued to push him.

"I thought you said he had a heart attack."

Wayne checked himself and hesitated before responding. He seemed to be on the point of lifting the barriers, and then I could tell they were once more coming down like a guillotine cutting off his real feelings.

"Yes, yes, he did, sort of." Wayne said hurriedly, dodging the issues like bullets from a machine gun. "The bath was removed and the bathroom was completely modernised and redecorated shortly after from the proceeds of Dad's insurance."

"Seems a desperate move. None of this quite adds up to a heart attack," I ventured.

"I don't know how she could live with her conscience." Wayne looked down shaking his head.

My doubt about the entry in the death certificate was really beginning to bug me and the coroner's connection with Inspector Fuller, that Rob had mentioned, was becoming somewhat more meaningful now.

"You know I was present when they removed my Dad from the bath." Wayne interrupted my thoughts.

"So, he had a heart attack in the bath?" I began to press him for an answer.

Wayne looked unsure of himself and hesitated again without answering.

"Look, Charlie, I'll be very frank with you, I don't particularly want to continue this line of questioning. I am finding this very painful and don't want to pursue this right now. But all I can say for now is that my father didn't look like someone who had just had a heart attack; still less a natural death."

At this point I could feel Wayne would not be pushed further on the details of his father's demise. He had had enough.

"So, what about the life insurance money?" I asked, easing off from the subject rather than push Wayne at this point.

"Are you kiddin'?" Wayne responded as if this too was a loaded question. "I would call it *hush money*."

"Can I ask you what the *hush* was about?" I asked tentatively.

The answer was not forthcoming and he skipped over the reasons and cut to the chase.

"I just couldn't face my mother anymore. I just packed and left in haste, accidentally leaving my address book and notes. It was a small price to pay to escape my mother's dominance over my life. That was it for me."

Eventually he broke a pained silence.

"Thanks again for returning my notes and address book," he said.

And by way of recovering from the emotional effects of our conversation he just asked how I managed to decode my notes?

"My secretary, Gloria worked out that some of it was Pitman's shorthand but we deciphered it in confidence," I assured him.

"I want you to know that nothing in your notebook has been revealed to your mother and that I told her that the coded wording was just brief notes that had little meaning."

There was visible relief on Wayne's face hearing that details in his notebook still remained his personal notes and his mother had not had the presence of mind to take it further.

"I'd like to call it a day," Wayne suggested, "but when I feel a bit stronger around this subject, perhaps we can meet up again soon. Perhaps same time tomorrow if I'm in the right frame of mind."

In all fairness it was getting late and the conversation around his father was proving to be quite stressful for Wayne.

"That's fine by me," I commiserated. "I know it's hard to live through moments like this without feeling drained."

I certainly couldn't complain. We had got nearer to the truth than before and I felt quite privileged that Wayne was talking to me like a friend. We seemed to have formed a bond. As for any allegiance to Mrs Saunders that was waning fast.

I left Wayne feeling a little guilty that I was leaving him in a somewhat vulnerable state and that I may have touched a nerve.

I hoped he didn't regret having spoken to me.

CHAPTER THIRTY

The piercing screams came from upstairs. The bathroom door open; one hand clinging grimly to the side of the bath and the other arm stiffly stretched out desperately grasping the air.

*****

Back in my apartment room I pondered over the mention of *hush money* which was dropped pretty quickly by Wayne. As I told myself before, it was the *elephant in the room*. I felt I needed to do a little more digging into it at a later date.

Meanwhile, my thoughts returned to Diana Saunders. The fact that she was here in Tinsel Town without even telling me made me feel I was being used, perhaps even as a decoy, like a gumshoe stooge in a Raymond Chandler novel.

Rob, to his credit, had followed up our last phone call with some information and photographic evidence on Fuller. This convinced me even more that the ever present Inspector was involved up to his neck in whatever Diana Saunders was hiding.

*****

The following day, as arranged with Wayne, I drove up the steep hill to Miller Drive and parked outside his house. Wayne seemed in good spirits as he greeted me, and with a wave of his hand he gestured me into the house.

"Come on in," he said, putting on his best American accent. It was hard to believe he was actually a boy from Willesden in North West London.

"Follow me," he said indicating the short winding staircase that led to the deck. Inwardly my heart sank as I had recurring visions of the whole thing collapsing. That being said, the outlook was certainly impressive. The smog was less evident today and there was a much clearer view of downtown Los Angeles.

"Come and see the garden. Don't look down, as Edmund Hillary said to Tensing Norgay at the summit of Everest!" Wayne joked as he led the way ever downwards.

"Let me show you what I do when I'm not in front of cameras," Wayne smiled encouragingly as we clambered down an incline of soft earth to the garden area beneath the wooden structure.

Looking back he could see that I was feeling anxious as I noticed above us the aging, creaking timber that was holding up the deck. Wayne clearly was enjoying my anxiety. I could only respond with a nervous smile.

Eventually we arrived at the bottom which with its steep incline seemed scarcely less precarious than the deck itself.

"So this is my garden," Wayne said proudly as he extended his hand to a well-kept space populated by neat grass and carefully arranged flowers.

"Very impressive," I said apprehensively. It may well have been but all I could picture was if the deck above us should start to fall we would both end up splashing into the neighbour's swimming pool below, that's if a tree didn't break our backs on the way down!

"It's certainly a nice view but do you mind if we go back upstairs my vertigo has gone into overdrive," I managed. My voice was shaking almost as much as I imagined was happening to the deck.

"Oh, sorry, I wasn't thinking." Wayne obliged and with some relief on my part, we headed back for the relative safety of the deck.

"You never told me how you got your first break in films," I said as we climbed the creaking stairway in an attempt to take my mind off the yawning abyss below.

"Funnily enough my first break was actually when I met a guy in a petrol station," Wayne revealed. "We started chatting whilst waiting for the attendant to fill our cars with 'gas'. This guy was making a movie but was short of an English sailor. Well, I dropped my American accent and told him to look no further, as here was an Englishman that had been in the Royal Navy!"

We arrived back in the house much to my relief.

"What a great story," I remarked as I exhaled with relief. "What happened then?"

"It was through my relationship with Raymond Quincy and those rather exotic poses that I showed you the other day that furthered my career." Wayne continued, "Raymond's hallmark was erotic representations of male nudes and he earned a reputation as a portrait artist of the rich and famous, including the Hollywood set. It naturally attracted me towards him as although I hate to admit it, it's a bit dog eat dog out here," Wayne disclosed. "I then moved to what seemed a step up the ladder via modelling, through the best beefcake magazine at the time, *Physique Pictorial* where I appeared on a few of the covers. I was very much into body building at the time and I found adverts galore down the gym where I worked out."

"Well it certainly seemed to pay off," I said admiringly.

"Oh yes," Wayne reminisced. "It was the start of being discovered for 'extra' work," Wayne assured me.

"How did they pick you out?" I enquired.

"Movie scouts would go round to the gyms and check out various venues for people who fitted the parts for their films. I was absolutely blown away when I got my first job as a slave in a 'B' movie and all I had to do was stand around in a loin cloth," Wayne laughed. "And got paid handsomely for it too!"

"Your mother said you got to know Marilyn Monroe. Was Diana just name dropping, or was that part true?" I asked.

"Oh it's true alright," Wayne assured me. "I started moving in the right circles and got into Paramount Studios. I had a few small parts in *The Ten Commandments* after being picked to model various costumes that Yul Brynner wore. We had a similar physique so I got noticed and was moved from modelling to finding myself in that movie."

"Did you move to Twentieth Century Fox after that?" It had been mentioned in his notebook.

"You've certainly done your research well," Wayne nodded. "I was recommended to move there and straightaway I got a part in

Gentlemen Prefer Blondes.   I was one of the extras in the Olympic Scene. We had to just stand around looking gorgeous next to Marilyn or pumping iron in the background and even diving over the head of Jane Russell."

He seemed to remember the scenes with obvious joy.

"So it's true, you did rub shoulders with Marilyn Monroe," I suggested enviously.

"A bit more than the shoulders, I'd say," Wayne chuckled.   "In fact, a year later I appeared in *There's No Business Like Showbusiness,* when I was aptly cast as a Tattooed Sailor.   I just had to stand there biceps on show while Ethel Merman, Marilyn Monroe and Mitzi Gaynor walked around me singing *A Sailor's Not a Sailor ('Til a Sailor's Been Tattooed).* Talk about going back to your roots."

Wayne looked at me with a knowing wink.

"Nice work if you can get it," I smiled broadly.

"You just have to get one foot in the door and in my case, my body and the world's your oyster," he said raising his eyebrows. "Hooking up with Rita had a lot to do with it too. Her Club was a road to fame and between us, we met a lot of the Hollywood stars. Fancy another coffee?" he offered.

"Yes please," I said, handing him my cup. "Were you in touch with Lester at this time?"

I really wanted to know a little more about the relationship between the brothers and when it started to crumble.

"Oh what a fuss Ma made of him, on his first leave from the RAF." Wayne shook his head disconsolately.

"I suppose I was envious of him and must admit, we lost contact once I moved out here to the States. Now I think back I realise it wasn't our fight. Lester ended up losing out because Ma took over his family life and he lost his wife and children. On the other hand, I escaped for a life on the ocean wave, distant lands and a smart uniform that I was proud to wear. There really was a girl in every port so what more could a hot-blooded male want?"

There was a cynical tone to the last remark and before I could ask anything more Wayne signalled it was time to stop.

"I'll tell you what Charlie, do you mind if we have a break?" Wayne stood to indicate that it was time for me to leave. "I've got another appointment shortly."

"No problem," I complied easily

"Hey, perhaps we can meet on Sunset Boulevard and take a walk on the Strip next time," he suggested.

"That would be great," I said thinking it would make a nice change and a chance to see where Wayne used to hang out when he first arrived here in Tinsel Town.

"Let's meet in a couple of days' time," Wayne concluded as he ushered me to the door.

PART THREE – SUNSET STRIP

CHAPTER THIRTY-ONE

It was time to check in with the office. Thankfully Gloria was holding the fort for me and answered the phone almost right away.

"All quiet on the western front," she assured me. "How are you getting on over there?"

"This western front is not so quiet here," I said. "You'll never guess who I've seen here in Los Angeles?"

"My favourite actor, Paul Newman and he wants to meet me!" she glibly remarked.

"No," I replied somewhat dejectedly. "It's far darker and more serious than that. I saw Mrs Saunders and a man I suspected was Inspector Fuller at one of the studios where Wayne used to work."

Even over the phone, across the great distance, I could hear Gloria audibly gasp.

"What on earth are they doing in America?" she asked catching her breath.

"I wish I knew," I replied in a slightly resigned tone.

"Rob's been checking Fuller out. Our intrepid Inspector is proving to be much more involved with Mrs S than I ever realised. I thought I'd been hired to find Wayne and get her money back but I'm fast beginning to realise it's just the tip of the iceberg. It's more about hush money and the reason for the 'hush'."

"Really?" Gloria exclaimed as if finding herself on the inside of some Hollywood detective movie. "What's Wayne like now you've got to meet him? Good guy? Bad guy?" Gloria was pushing for an answer.

"He's turning out to be the good guy. His mother though...." I paused. "She's turning out to be a female Jekyll and Hyde character."

I decided I needed to confide in Gloria as there was nobody else.

"Gloria, I've ended up in such a dilemma," I confessed.

"Why?" Gloria seemed confused. "What's the dilemma?"

"To start with I couldn't make up my mind when or if to tell Wayne that not only was I working for his mother but I had seen her here in LA."

"I hope you decided to tell him," Gloria responded sharply in her usual direct manner. "You know you would regret it if she finds where he is and turns up on his doorstep."

"I absolutely dreaded telling him," I continued as if it was a confessional. "Don't forget there is client confidentiality to keep in mind."

"Oh come on," Gloria scolded. "Get a grip Charlie, don't keep me on tenterhooks. What did you decide?"

"Simply because Mrs Saunders was not playing straight with me, I decided to tell him she was here," I said. "I actually felt she was using me to get to Wayne but in a very duplicitous way. I didn't like it."

"How did Wayne react when you told him?" Gloria enquired.

"He was understandably shocked but it helped him open up a bit more about the circumstances around his father's death," I continued.

"He had a heart attack, didn't he?" Gloria recalled.

"He keeps avoiding saying anything much about it.   I have this gut feeling there's more to his father's death, than meets the eye," I confided.

"So how do you feel about still working for Mrs Saunders," Gloria asked.

"I don't," I said emphatically.

"Well, keep me posted, please," Gloria insisted.

We ended comparing the weather, as you do.   Sunny California versus raining and grey London. Some things never change.

"Call you in a few days," I said ending the call.

*****

I took the rest of the day off to look around the surrounding area and drove over to Grauman's Chinese Theatre a movie palace on the historic Hollywood Walk of Fame on Hollywood Boulevard in Hollywood. I walked over the concrete blocks set in the forecourt, checking out the signatures, footprints, and handprints of popular motion picture personalities.   Apparently the origins of the footprints may well have been an accident when someone stepped into the wet concrete whilst it was being built.

The theatre itself dated back to 1927 and grew to become a tourist attraction. It was nice to be a tourist and I enjoyed reading the famous names imprinted in the concrete like Mary Pickford and Douglas Fairbanks.

It gave me something else to think about, other than Diana Saunders appearance in LA.

*****

CHAPTER THIRTY-TWO

"What's the matter? Wet your bed, Jew boy?"

"If you want to take a piss, Saunders, go to the head like the rest of us do."

"He's a Jew boy, alright, he's circumcised."

"Jew boy, you'd better go home to your mother."

"You can always sleep with Dusty Miller, you know…"

*****

As arranged with Wayne, a couple of days later, he met me outside *Ciro*'s at the bottom of the hill on the corner, which saved me walking up to Miller Drive. Wayne did not seem to find the gradient quite as daunting as I did but then he was a lot fitter than me. He would run up and down that hill on a daily basis like a Whippet up a drainpipe just to keep fit. For me that would be torture.

"I've been thinking about the appearance of my mother," he said as we walked to the diner. "It does bother me but there's not a lot I can do about it. In fact, perhaps this may lead to an inevitable showdown."

"I'm sorry you have had to go through all of this," I apologised looking over at Wayne.

"No, please don't apologise," Wayne said with certainty. "I feel this was meant to be and will cross my mother's bridge when I get to it."

Wayne looked down thoughtfully as we walked along the Strip.

Before too long we saw a sign that promised the "best Belgian waffles in LA". So enticed we entered and found a good place to sit and started looking down the menu. A waitress came over to take our order reminding me of Lana Turner in the film *Slightly Dangerous*.

Actually it was her outfit that caught my eye. Unlike the waitresses back home, she wore a smart short-sleeved pink gingham dress worn just above the knees, with a white petticoat apron, all set off with something resembling a nurse's hat on her head.

She had my attention and no mistake.

"How did you get on in the Navy?" I asked, reluctantly turning my attention to Wayne as the attractive waitress in her pink gingham dress walked away.

"I sort of kept myself to myself whilst I was in the Navy as I wasn't too good at socialising," Wayne began almost by way of apology. "I remember how I learned chores like spud peeling, cleaning out the head and other such delicate jobs, which the Navy was expert in finding. I even learned how to put polish on and shine my shoes, as well as bedmaking with folded ends, folded tops, six inches turned here, eight inches tucked under there."

Watching Wayne's thin smile, I could see that in hindsight it was a pleasant memory, one that he knew his mother wouldn't believe but Geraldine would have appreciated.

It wasn't long, however, that Wayne's tale of Naval life turned to a much darker side.

"We had a naval chaperone, Dusty Miller was his name," Wayne reminisced. "The other lads thought he was 'queer' cos of the way they said he looked at the boys in the shower. He was called an 'arsehole fucker' and the usual banter about size. But then I remember the cursing moving onto them talking about hating kikes, queers and niggers but I managed to stay out of conversations most of the time to avoid the prejudice talk."

Wayne hesitated as if the memory was actually quite painful.

"But sometimes it wasn't easy to avoid," Wayne continued after a while. "One time the lads found out that our Leader was Jewish. They thought he was a pretty good egg but when they heard he was Jewish their opinion of him suddenly changed. They had a stereotypical point of view of a Jew; selfish, loaded and a big nose. When I stuck up for the Leader saying he was still a good teacher, they turned on me and called me a Jew lover and I remember they invited me to screw Leader and get married!"

"The usual reliance on petty but hostile language," I added.

"They wondered why I was sticking up for Leader," Wayne nodded. "They questioned whether I was Jewish. It had never occurred to them that I might be. They wanted me to prove I was Jewish by saying something in Jewish! I think that more or less sums up their intelligence. Thank goodness, I was saved by any further awkwardness by the deep heavy voice of the Squadron Regulating Petty Officer resounding from outside the dormitory."

Wayne told me this was just the beginning of the type of antisemitism there was in the Services. He found it astounding that a Jew was defined by a big nose and wads of money.

"Things just don't seem to improve, we just don't learn," I frowned.

"That's an understatement!" Wayne was adamant and continued. "One night I got dressed up to go out. One of the lads said I looked like I was going to church. I opened my mouth before engaging my brain and just calmly turned round and said: 'I don't go to church…. I'm Jewish'. It was a bad move."

*****

Our waffles arrived courtesy of our waitress and we tucked in. As she walked away with a Hollywood swaying of the hips we tucked into the waffles, which I have to admit were the best I'd ever tasted.

Wayne hesitated before continuing, clearly this was going to be a bitter memory.

"It was only when I started to return back to camp, I recalled that slip of the tongue and wondered what sort of welcome I was going to get. On top of that, it started to rain that night so I skipped the cinema and decided to head back to camp and get a good night's rest."

There was a further pause while Wayne concentrated on his waffle and considered the memory of that particular incident.

"What happened then?" I coaxed almost fearful of the response.

"I entered the dormitory and quietly got out of my navy blues and just jumped into the sack," he said. "As my body came into contact with the sheets, the lights went on and I found myself surrounded by grinning faces. Someone had dumped a bucket of water into my bed. That's when the name calling started."

He recalled the incident bitterly and verbatim remembering every sick word as if it were a nail hammered into his psyche. Clearly this experience had affected him badly and still cast its long distended shadow over his present bright and fairly positive life.

"It would have been easy to retaliate but I didn't want to provoke any physical violence," he said. "The taunts just kept coming until they got fed up. It was hard to stomach especially knowing that I was going to be fighting shoulder to shoulder with these men against the enemy. I had to ask myself who was the enemy?"

I really felt for Wayne in that moment knowing exactly where he was coming from. It sickened me and I wasn't even there at the time.

"What happened next?" I said expecting further repercussions.

"The following day, Dusty Miller called me into his office," Wayne continued. "He already knew exactly what had happened in the dormitory the night before. I thought he had called me in on some misdemeanour and was about to send me home. It turned out he was considering sending me to Officer Training School."

"Wow! That was a turn up for the books," I exclaimed relieved that the story had a more positive outcome.

"I was so grateful to find someone was on my side," Wayne said visibly brightening. "Miller showed me real understanding about the situation and how I felt about myself. He sent me up ahead of the class to my new base. I don't think I would have got through the Navy without Miller. At last I found someone who had faith in me."

CHAPTER THIRTY-THREE

We finished our waffles and Wayne invited me to walk further up Sunset Strip to the Sunset Colonial Hotel. He said he had arranged to meet a pal of his and was happy for me to join them.

It turned out to be a nice opportunity to meet Vanoye Aitkens, a close friend who knew Wayne from his arrival in Los Angeles.

We walked to the restaurant and sitting at a table was a poised, black gentleman.

"Well, hello handsome," this supple-looking guy stood up, batting his eyelids at me and pursing his lips in a faux kiss.

"Hello, I'm Charlie Moray, nice to meet you," I said in my best English accent and exaggerated masculinity.

"You can call me Van," he said in a smouldering sort of way whilst extending a well-manicured hand. I shook his hand almost shyly. I was not used to this outward display of masculine affection as he turned to Wayne and gave him a tender 'man hug'.

Van did not hold back as we all sat down and he proceeded to do a one-man fan base for Wayne.

"You know, Wayne was in the 1952 version of *The Ten Commandments*," Van boasted for Wayne. "Go on, Wayne, tell him what you did on that movie."

"I already have," Wayne said firmly.

"Did you mention standing in front of Cecil B de Mille in a leather thong and not much else?" Van added mischievously in a high-pitched voice. "Not a lot of people can boast that statement!"

"I was a 'body stand-in' for Yul Brynner in the movie because we had similar physiques." Wayne explained even though I'd heard the story before. "I was in *The Ten Commandments* as a slave, a centurion and any parts where a 'body' was required. I was even one of the first to get through the parting of the Red Sea!"

Wayne laughed.

"You played a lot of roles where someone in a loin cloth was required!" Van reminded him with approval.

"*The Ten Commandments* was truly my big break," Wayne proclaimed, "but then I've already told Charlie that."

"I was a distant admirer of Wayne," Van chimed in, looking over at Wayne. "In fact, we met at this very place back then. Wayne caught my eye, and we've been friends ever since," he added with affection. "We were both at the start of our careers."

Wayne intervened in a more restrained manner. "Van was known as a flamboyant dancer. You may not know Katherine Dunham but she created the Dunham Technique and Van became her dancing partner."

"Her technique transformed the world of dance," Van resumed his story with a delicate wave of his hand. "I'm obviously older than I look, but in the 40's I danced with Katherine at the Prince of Wales Theatre in London."

I assumed that the London connection gave Wayne and Van something in common from the start.

"Is it safe to say that entry into Hollywood at that time, was by way of the modelling scene?" I asked both of them.

"Well it wasn't for his excellent memory!" Van said immediately looking over at Wayne then threw back his head and laughed. "The only reason Wayne didn't make it as an acclaimed actor was because he couldn't remember his lines!"

"That's unfortunately true," Wayne admitted. "In actual fact, a lot of my time was taken up with body building. I was finding that my physique opened doors and I got to know all the Chiefs of Casting. It was the equivalent of the casting couch for men!"

"Hmmm," Van pursed his lips in agreement. "We were climbing the ladder more or less at the same time. There were those photographs you did for *Physique Pictorial* as I recall, dear." Van had resumed a mischievous tone, titling his head to one side and raising his eyebrows.

"Admittedly it was the exotic poses on the cover of *Physique Pictorial* that opened a few doors for me," Wayne conceded. "A little like the poses I did for Raymond Quincy which I'll show you, Charlie."

Caught unawares, I just nodded more in embarrassment than anything else.

For no apparent reason, it suddenly struck me that Diana Saunders could so easily stroll past the diner and I started to feel anxious and uneasy. I also thought she may have extracted Wayne's address from the studios as she was a relative.

I was brought out of my paranoid thoughts.

"Has Wayne mentioned his partnership with Raymond Quincy and his naked men in erotic poses?" Van giggled and then laughed openly.

"Yes," I answered rather quickly, catching the mood. "I've heard about them!"

"Quite revealing weren't they darling?" Van looked over at Wayne.

"Oh come on, Van," Wayne gently shoved Van.

"Gosh, look at the time!" Van exclaimed. "I've got to get to another appointment. It's been good to meet you Charlie, but I must dash."

"It's been good to meet you too, Van," I smiled a little awkwardly. "You've been most entertaining. I hope we get to meet up again before I leave."

"How did we get through the whole meet up without even a mention of your mother?" Van added as he looked over at Wayne with a lift of one eyebrow.

At that Van turned, and with a flourish of his scarf, he sashayed away into the bright sunlight of a Hollywood afternoon.

CHAPTER THIRTY-FOUR

Replenished by the waffles and Van's added frivolity, Wayne and I returned to Miller Drive.

"Come on Charlie, I'll show you the paintings I posed for Raymond Quincy," Wayne said as we entered his abode.

I followed Wayne through to the second bedroom and there were the paintings taking up half the wall. I tried not to stare but to say these were erotic poses was something of an understatement. I couldn't help myself. To tell the truth I wasn't sure where to look!

"Here's one of the most famous, *The Aztec Sacrifice*," Wayne announced.

"Looks a bit like an exotic suspended star jump!" I muffled an uncomfortable laugh.

"If you had been hanging up like that for a fair amount of hours, you wouldn't find it so amusing; I was exhausted," Wayne replied with a smile.

"One helluva way to earn a living," I ventured.

"True," Wayne responded. "It began as a modelling job at Raymond's Fine Arts Studios in Los Angeles. Raymond was 20 years older than me and I was a young, eager guy looking to get into the right crowd. I became his muse and yes, before you ask, we were lovers too. The *Aztec Sacrifice* is just one of many I posed for him and still fetches a fair price now."

The next bit was going to be a bit awkward.

"I hope I'm not giving away any confidences but Guy did mention your partnership with Raymond Quincy," I added nervously after a while. I decided not to mention that friends called Wayne a "gold digger" after Raymond kicked him out in a fit of pique. The relationship went sour and Raymond had angrily removed Wayne's name out on all the business stationery.

"It's a difficult time being homosexual," Wayne explained. "It is illegal and we are still almost in hiding. Sodomy is a crime and a person can be convicted and imprisoned for up to 20 years. We are still being stigmatised to this day."

The temperature had dropped outside and matched the chill in the conversation. Wayne had been opening up to me, but now he seemed strangely reluctant to proceed. I felt I knew him enough by now to drop the subject.

Wayne waited a while before piping up again.

"That's it then, let's take a trip to Las Vegas for a few days," he abruptly declared out of the blue. "I feel I need to get away. The fact that my mother's in the vicinity makes me feel uneasy and I'd rather not be at home if she turns up."

He seemed resigned to the fact that a visit from his mother was not only inevitable, but imminent.

"Do you think Rita might like to join us?" I said avoiding further reference to the presence of his mother.

"She could do with a break and she's great company," Wayne said. "I'll give her a call shortly. She's quite impulsive, so I'm sure she'll drop everything and come along."

"You might like to forewarn her that your mother's in town," I remarked.

"Agreed," Wayne concluded. "I don't think she'll be too impressed."

***

Later that evening, Wayne called me.

"Rita's furious," Wayne exclaimed. "She was shouting hysterically down the phone asking me what the hell was going on."

I felt contrite that I had put Wayne in an unenviable position.

"I'm really sorry Wayne," I admitted shamefully. "I feel this is my fault, especially as I saw her at the studios a few days ago and I was torn between telling you or not."

"Well Rita just couldn't believe it and she isn't too happy I can tell you," Wayne said.

"Is she still going to come with us to Las Vegas," I asked hopefully, "or have I spoiled everything?"

"I told her that you have dropped my mother as a client and that you've actually helped me come to terms with some things," Wayne added in a lighter tone. "She was much calmer by the end of our conversation and in fact, she is even more keen to come with us. Women? I don't even try to understand them."

I had to grin at that one.

This wasn't really the way we wanted to start our trip to Las Vegas but it could have overcast the entire journey like a shadow. This way there was nothing hidden and some of the mystery had been revealed.

PART FOUR – ROUTE 66

CHAPTER THIRTY–FIVE

I rang the doorbell to Wayne's house, slightly apprehensive as to how Rita might react. I hadn't seen her since I spotted Diana Saunders at the studios with her pet Detective in tow and wasn't sure if she still blamed me for leading this awful poisonous woman to Wayne's doorstep.

The door opened immediately and there was Wayne standing there.

"Right! Come on in," he said with what sounded like false enthusiasm. "Ding dong the witch is dead, only bad memories. Let's leave them behind and follow the yellow brick road."

Rita was already inside and to my relief greeted me with less hostility than I had anticipated. She did grill me for a short time but that was to be expected. I managed to convince her that I had now worked out whose side I was on and would try and protect Wayne from any confrontation should his mother and her keeper appear.

"I was a mug and I admit it," I said by way of contrition.

Rita gave me what might be called an old fashioned look. That said she seemed to be reassured that it was all out in the open and we were going to have a good trip.

"Life's too short, let's enjoy it." Rita brought the issue to an abrupt close as we left Miller Drive and piled into Wayne's spacious and classy Chrysler.

*****

The top of the Chrysler was down and the road stretched out in front of us seemingly forever. On each side of its hot tarmac ribbon, there was a vast and dusty, desert terrain, with a beautiful mountainous backdrop, along the main highway of the legendary Route 66.

They could make out the horizon in the near distance through the heat haze turning the road into a liquid mirage.

On leaving Los Angeles, the three of us had remained quietly preoccupied with our own thoughts but with the city at our backs, the atmosphere lifted. Slowly we all began to relax and forget about the presence of Diana Saunders and the dark shadow she continued to cast over Wayne's life.

I had a captive audience, trapped in the spacious confines of the Chrysler with miles of desert ahead of us. Hoping this would ease the strain and open up a good atmosphere I ventured to open a conversation on a lighter tone.

"There's a reference to an engagement in your diary Wayne," I said looking at Rita.

"Rita, were you and Wayne really engaged?"

Rita smiled awkwardly but looked ahead in the passenger seat seemingly unable to retain my gaze.

"I scratched Wayne's back and he applied the itch repellent to mine!" she continued to smile.

I felt relieved that Rita was taking this relatively well.

"It was a purely mutual and business-like relationship," Wayne chimed in with a light smile on his lips looking around at Rita.

"I had just started up the nightclub," Rita returned the look. "I needed to build up a good clientele. Wayne and I were instantly attracted to each other, but in different ways. I could also see that Wayne had an eye for the Producers and was beginning to get himself small parts in the 'movies'. He invited celebrities he met to the club and his English accent was quite a novelty back then. We were a good team and as you can see, we still are."

Rita paused before giving Wayne a cheeky look. "We are forever engaged," she winked at him. "He loves boys and I love gals!"

So there we have it I thought.

"Damn, my secret is out," Wayne said with mock anguish, "how am I ever to go on, now?"

*****

As the heat began to climb on the drive, we decided to put the top back up for shade from the sun and switch on the air conditioning. However, this was short lived. We had been enjoying the air-conditioned environment of the Chrysler as the miles went by, when we spotted an encrusted sign "Switch Off Air Conditioning" which appeared out of the dust, by the side of the road.

"This heat reminds me of the time on HMS Illustrious when I was still a Scribe." Wayne said mopping his brow. "It was made entirely of steel and in cold weather it was like living in a king-sized refrigerator and in the heat, it was like an oven, a bit like now!"

The miles had clocked up and it was time to take a break from the road to Las Vegas. We stopped off at the Silver Dollar for a drink and slight relief from the searing heat outside.

Refreshed once again, we got back into the car and Rita and I shared the drive onwards passing through the Painted Desert and near the Grand Canyon. It was like driving through a moonscape of dunes and emptiness stretching as far as the eye could see and then beyond.

I was itching to ask Wayne about the Corsair operation as there was an entry in his diary and also the letter the Royal Navy had forwarded to me.

"Wayne," I asked at last, "any chance you can tell us about the Corsair operation if Rita hasn't heard the story."

Rita nodded an agreement and Wayne began to tell his tale.

*****

<u>OPERATION MERIDIAN -</u> *Quonset Point, Rhode Island - <u>(factual event refer pp330-331)</u>*

Wayne was a Secretary to the Commanding Officer with what he described as sub-standard typing. As for the Commanding Officer, he was a hard strait-laced, brusque man, affectionately known as Commander Ironside amongst the ranks. Wayne found the Corsairs fascinating sitting on the aprons, with wings that would fold up. The first flights were made by the new pilots on the Squadron. Describing the scene to me he remembered watching for the ten Corsairs to return to base. However, only nine aircraft had landed.

The next day Wayne counted the Corsairs in. Four of them made bad landings, the fifth one almost hit the runway. The sixth, seventh and eighth planes landed without incident but then they waited for number nine.

Eventually, Wayne took it upon himself to send a wire reporting another plane and pilot lost. Word had got around and now several of the pilots were feeling quite scared about going up. Ironside had assured him that an investigation was taking place but that didn't quell the feeling of fear among the young men.

They had still been waiting for the results of the investigation when disaster hit like lightning striking twice. The pilots got into their cockpits and eight of them taxied out on the runway and took off.

A plane was already in trouble.

Before Wayne or anyone else knew anything about it fire engines and an ambulance tore across the apron to the end of the runway.

Wayne was counting them back in… one, two, three, came in. As number four came into view it started to spin. Then, five and six came in and they were waiting for the seventh one which never appeared.

Wayne picked up the narrative.

"Send a Wire to the Commanding officer, British Squadrons, Washington DC," Ironside said. "Report that one of the planes suddenly went into a spin and crash-landed into the ocean."

"To add to the tragedy the Corsair had been flown by a young pilot who had just married before he left England. As Scribe I had to type out a form A7 with 3 carbon copies – *Loss of Life of Naval*. I remember my hands shook as I inserted them between the four official forms and placed them in the typewriter. I typed his name, rank and next of kin and all the other details required. Then I had to fill in the details under 'Reason for Loss of Naval Officer.' Did it matter now whether it was the war, disgust, a faulty plane? I thought, what the hell, who's even going to bother? All that was left of this young lad was 4 sheets of paper, not even a decent burial."

The report from the Commanding Officer stated that the pilot had *failed to lock and secure his right wing before take-off. His wing held until an undeterminable height, then wing started to fold and plane crashed into sea. Loss is attributable to negligence of pilot.*

"Even in death, this poor young lad was blamed."

*****

"My goodness," Rita said, clearly touched by the account. That's horrendous. You never really hear about these tragedies do you?"

"No," Wayne responded with an edge of bitterness in his voice. "It was all hush-hush and Top Secret at the time. In the end, following the investigation, all planes were grounded and there was some relief but the problem had still not been resolved. It was then to our surprise, that Ironside decided to take up a plane."

"He was brave," Rita observed.

"He certainly was," Wayne replied with admiration and respect both in his voice and on his suntanned face. "We waited nervously for his plane to return. I can't tell you how relieved and elated we were when we saw the Corsair appear. Later that day, Ironside dictated a letter to the Commanding Officer in Washington stating he had resolved the major problem that was causing the Corsair to crash."

"What was the result?" Rita was really absorbed in this encounter.

"He discovered that when the plane reached a certain height, poisonous fumes were seeping into the cockpit," Wayne explained. "This answered the question as to the reason why those poor pilots never responded. They were unconscious."

"How terrible and such a waste of young lives," Rita shook her head in despair. "But how would he have known that about the fumes?" she queried.

"Ironside suspected there was some escape of poisonous gas so he took a special mask with him and container of oxygen," Wayne continued to explain. "As soon as he noticed traces of carbon monoxide, he put the mask on. His recommendation was to incorporate a special adjustment to the engine to eliminate the poisonous gas and that saved so many pilots in the future."

"Wow, what a hero," I exclaimed.

"He was, but sadly shortlived." Wayne's tone became sombre. "I was still with 1830 Squadron on HMS Illustrious when an apprentice Batting Officer was taking command of the landings. Old Ironside was flying in but this apprentice waved him off four times and we could see he was getting really angry. When Ironside came in for a fifth approach, he decided enough was enough. He would do it his way and ignore the directions of the Batting Officer to come lower. Ironside cut the engines but we could see he would miss the trip wires and go crashing into the first barrier and head for the parked planes. Suddenly he saw the error of his ways."

"How awful," Rita exclaimed. "So what did he do?"

"He knew he'd made a mistake but it was too late to rectify it," Wayne recalled clearly remembering the disastrous outcome.

"We could hear the engine starting to rev and catch and the plane began to climb but then the engine cut out completely over the port side of the ship."

Wayne continued visualising the event. "The left wing struck a pom-pom position and Ironside opened his cockpit. We could see him desperately punching his fist to his stomach to release himself but the plane spun over and into the ocean. Three loud bursts from the fog-horn of the Illustrious brought the two escorting Destroyers over to the scene. It really was tragic. There wasn't a sign of the plane or pilot as the wash from the ships billowed right over the mark. I couldn't believe my eyes. Just a matter of moments ago, I had been talking to him. I went over to one of the mechanics, who confirmed there was no sign of Ironside. I was stunned and just said to myself 'he's gone'. Then one of the mechanics turned to me and said that Ironside wasn't supposed to fly that day. It made me think the cruel hand of fate can sometimes be so harsh.

It was true. In fact, Ironside was in such a foul mood that day and insisted on being put down to fly. We knew that his plane had only just completed its thousand mile check out, and hadn't been washed and cleaned the way he liked it. But he was so insistent to be put on the flight schedule, or else! Even in that awful moment, I couldn't help thinking that Ironside and my Ma would have made a pretty good pair being so good at giving out orders!"

Rita and I tried to take in the gravity of an event that never hit the headlines.

Bereft of speech we simply looked out at the parched horizon and sat in silence as the big Chrysler consumed yet more miles of empty desert road.

Eventually Rita broke the silence by switching on the radio.

"Let's have some music," Rita cheerfully announced.

The soundtrack was provided by Frank Sinatra singing *Fly Me to the Moon*."

"How very apt," I said pondering the desert landscape. "It feels like we're travelling on the moon right now."

CHAPTER THIRTY-SIX

"Come on now, I'll see you to the door," she told her son, eager for him to leave.

They walked to the door together. She opened the door catch and put her cheek next to Wayne's lips, expecting a kiss.

"Now be a good boy and don't go getting yourself into any mischief."

Those were his mother's farewell words as she shut the door firmly behind him. He slowly started to descend the long, dark staircase. Unable to hold it back, his eyes filled with tears which he desperately tried to hold back – but they just flowed and flowed.

*****

We remained in silence as I drove for yet more miles just taking in the vast and dusty landscape. On the radio which was proving a godsend, we listened to a mixture of music from Louis Armstrong to Billie Holliday and some of the great crooners of the time.

Eventually we pulled up and Rita decided to take over the driving. I moved to the passenger seat and Wayne reclined in the back.

"I think you'll agree with me, Charlie, that London's Terminal Stations are pretty dismal at the best of times," he recalled with a poignant smile. "They're dirty and dreary places and Waterloo is the worst of the bunch! There was only one class on the trains; first and third had been eliminated. The prosperous were forced to mix with poor, peers with peasants, lords with labourers and officers with enlisted personnel."

Wayne it seemed was once more reminiscing about his wartime experience and how wretched he felt on his departure to unknown territories.

"I found the platform where my train was to depart," he said with all the dejection he must have felt at the time. "There was no need to hang around. There was no-one coming to see me off, so I found a seat. It made it worse seeing people who cared enough to come to the station kissing and hugging each other not knowing whether they would see their loved ones ever again. I found a window seat and moved to a dimly lit part of the train, where I could pretend to sleep as it slowly began to move out of the station."

"Oh sweetheart," Rita sympathised with genuine concern. "You've never mentioned this before."

"I've tried to put it behind me and concentrate on my new life here," he looked up with sad eyes. "Once I got to my destination, I was fine. I took the Writer's Course and passed with fairly good marks. I decided that having had such a bad time when I stated I was Jewish, I would tell them I was Church of England to make life a lot simpler," he said with a knowing grin.

"Did your mum and Dad get in touch?" I ventured.

"I received a letter out of the blue. My father wrote to me saying that Ma was sick. I thought it might be a nice surprise to return home and see her. But the surprise was on me. There was no-one at home and I couldn't understand why my father had written to say Ma was sick when she was obviously out and about with him. It was all very strange and I couldn't wait to return to base. When I did return, I got sent to a secret destination. It was Scotland!"

I couldn't help but burst out laughing and Rita caught on that Scotland was nowhere exotic and couldn't be that far away.

"Only joking," Wayne continued. "We started off there but ended up in Egypt and there was talk of America too."

"Join the Navy and see the World," I made a poor attempt at a salute.

"I was the new Scribe but all I remember was throwing up constantly and I couldn't even 'fall in' on the first day," Wayne recalled. "I might have been in the Navy but I was a terrible sailor."

I grinned back at Wayne. I'd read somewhere that Horatio Nelson was seasick too.

CHAPTER THIRTY-SEVEN

We travelled on a few more miles feeling more upbeat and laughing at Wayne being a sailor and not able to even stand up on his first 'fall in'. However, this was to be far from his last journey at sea. Eventually and much as Saul took his road to Damascus, so Wayne arrived at the mouth of the Hudson on the HMS Queen Elizabeth and took his first step on the dry land of the New World.

The fantasy of New York had already started to become a reality to Wayne, even before the Statue of Liberty came into view with the iconic Manhattan skyline, at her back. However, his impressions of America were soon to be missed as the long Greyhound bus pulled out of the busy Metropolis to its destination, the Berkeley Hotel, Asbury Park, New Jersey.

"Nobody expected 1830 Squadron. There was no food ready for us," he recalled. "In the end an emergency meal had to be served. The base was completely run by the British and bacon and beans was all they could muster!"

"Let's face it American food is so much better," Rita chipped in.

Neither Wayne nor I could disagree with that.

"Actually I met a nice Jewish girl, Daphne, while we were stationed there and Jewish families do know how to eat," Wayne recalled this happy memory. "I found myself at their dinner table having matzo ball soup, roast chicken and lokshen pudding, I think they were trying to *schmooze* me for their daughter's sake. She was only 15 but she was much more experienced than I was."

"Oh really," Rita raised an eyebrow.

"I really had no idea," Wayne chuckled. "Her father reprimanded me for taking advantage of his daughter and did what my Dad didn't get to do, sit down with me and talk about the birds and the bees! I returned to base a lot wiser even though I ended up leaning towards the bees and the bees!"

"So you enjoyed the 'Big Apple', I asked.

"I certainly did," Wayne replied. "I didn't miss one tourist attraction that New York had to offer, squeezed into five days and then had to say goodbye to Daphne forever.

I looked around me. By my reckoning we were about midway between Los Angeles at our backs and Las Vegas before us but the city in the Nevada Desert was still nowhere in sight.

"Let's stop at the next place for a drink," Rita suggested, looking towards me and then you can take over the driving for a while, Charlie."

Eventually a sign said 'Dairy and Snack Bar' and we pulled up outside another quintessentially American diner. Inside the cool of the air conditioning was inviting and also something unfamiliar from my previous experience in England. We had no time restraints and sat at the nearby table where we ordered some drinks and snacks.

There were a few other people scattered around the tables who were also enjoying the break from their long drives and the relentless heat.

"What happened when you left America?" I asked Wayne.

"By that time, I was on HMS Slinger sailing into Liverpool and the whole Squadron was given ten days leave," he replied thinking back. "I struggled with my kit bag containing the rarities and luxuries I knew Ma would appreciate. It was November and I got into London greeted by a dismal cold, foggy, drizzling day.

"That's how we imagine England to always be like," Rita laughed.

"As Frank Sinatra would have it, *It's so nice to go travelling but oh so nice to come home*." However, I doubted that this was how Wayne saw things as a taxi cab took him from Victoria station to the Saunders household in Willesden.

"When I got home, nothing had changed," Wayne said miserably. "I kicked the gate, but it still hadn't been fixed, so I dropped my bags and familiarly lifted the lock from the other side and swaggered up the pathway in true Naval tradition."

CHAPTER THIRTY-EIGHT

"Anyone home?" Wayne shouted out as he entered the house.

"Is that you, Wayne?" his mother's voice came back to him.

"Yes, it's me," came the confirmation.

"Well, don't come upstairs for a minute, I don't have any clothes on. I'll be down soon."

Diana Saunders eventually came down the stairs in her well-tailored bathrobe.

"Damn sweets they make today, stick in your teeth," she said as she tried to dislodge a piece of candy from between her teeth with her thumb.

Wayne waited downstairs, looking around to see if anything had changed.

"Oh there you are Wayne. My you're looking good. They certainly look as if they fed you well over there. Was their cooking as good as mine?" she asked without waiting for an answer. As she walked past Wayne, her gaze dropped to his packages and kit bag.

"You've got so much baggage this time, I don't know why you drag all that nonsense home. Couldn't you leave some on the ship or barracks, instead of bringing it all here? I have enough to contend with at home.

Wayne stood in his uniform looking at his mother in sheer exasperation.

*****

"Hello Wayne," a familiar voice was heard behind him.

Wayne swung round, "Hey Lester, good to see you, when did you get in?"

"Two days ago. I've only got a week, think I'm going back to India but it's real hush-hush right now and no-one is supposed to know."

"Wish I knew what was going to happen to us," Wayne said to Lester. "Don't know if we'll swing around the buoy at Southampton, or if they'll send us to the Med. May even bump into you in India, who knows?"

Avoiding any further interruption from their mother, Wayne and Lester continued upstairs with their bags.

Once in the sanctity of their room, Wayne turned to Lester.

"I've got something for you here."

Wayne started to unpack his kitbag and brought out the 'booty' for Lester to see.

"Gosh, I haven't seen canned fruit in years and fresh bananas," Lester said.

"Cor! Worth their weight in gold. What's this? Cranberry sauce? What's that for?"

"They use that in America when they have turkey."

"Well, no wonder we don't have it here," Lester replied. "We never see turkey."

"There's more for you here," Wayne said, producing a carton of cigarettes and a bottle of After Shave.

"Are these strong?" Lester asked studying the soft pack of 20 Camel cigarettes.

"I don't know." Wayne replied. "I don't smoke but aren't smokes real hard to get here still?"

"Yeah," Lester replied moving onto the bottle which he studied quizzically. "And what's this After Shave Lotion?"

"Oh, it's out of this world," Wayne explained. "You just pat a little on your face right after you shave in the morning, it makes you feel great and has a very pleasant smell to it."

"You use it?" Lester asked his brother his eyebrows knitted into a frown.

"Sure."

"Well, you can keep it" Lester retorted. Only poofs and fairies would use perfume." Lester retorted.

"But all the men use it in America," Wayne protested anxiously.

"Well, they're nothing but a bunch of fairies in that case," Lester responded bluntly.

At that point, Mrs Saunders burst into the room, looking searchingly at her two sons.

"I've got a few things here for you… Ma." Wayne turned to her and produced a bunch of bananas, lemons and a package from his kitbag as if from a magician's hat.

"Are those silk stockings?" Diana enquired studying the package.

"No, they're nylons." Wayne said.

"Nylons?!" Diana looked curious.

"Yes, that's what the women are wearing in America now," Wayne explained. They last longer and are supposed to be more sheer than silk."

"Hmm, let me try them on." His mother took a pair and parting her long gown, showing her long shapely legs, slowly began to put the stockings on.

"Hmm, I like them. What do you think of them, Lester?"

"Oh, they look super-duper, Ma."

"How many pairs did you bring, Wayne?" she enquired.

"I could only get three pairs," he almost apologised. "They're very difficult to get hold of."

"And all this canned fruit," she continued. "Oh, I'm really going to knock Mrs. Ferguson's eyes out with this. Her son brought her back a box of tangerines last week. Wait till she gets a load of this. She's such a show off, I'll really make her bloody eyes pop out of her head. What else did you get Wayne?"

And that's exactly what she did. She went to her husband's Club and behind a special mesh partition, she flagrantly displayed all the fresh fruit and vegetables that Wayne had brought back from America. Casually thrown in *the background was a pair of stockings, a carton of American cigarettes and a bottle of After Shave Lotion.*

CHAPTER THIRTY-NINE

Our open top Chrysler consumed the miles to Las Vegas and as a cloak of darkness set on the desert, the city came finally into our sights.

"At last," Rita sounded relieved as the bright neon lights came into view.

We just drank in the sight of the Flamingo Hotel, The Desert Inn, The Sands Hotel and Casino, and Dunes heralding our arrival at Las Vegas.

"I'm happy to just check in and relax," I said and Rita and Wayne very quickly agreed.

We booked in for a two nights stay at the Flamingo, so we had time to relax and meet up in the morning for breakfast.

*****

I went to my room. I had a shower and put my feet up to relax when there was a knock on my door. I thought it might be room service but on opening, Wayne was standing outside.

"Charlie do you mind having a drink and a chat," he stood outside awkwardly.

"Well, I'm not going to be able to sleep straightaway," I said stepping aside, "so come on in." Wayne entered and I gestured for him to sit in the armchair by the window.

"Whatever my mother is paying you, I will top it in order to keep her out of my life," Wayne said sharply as he sat down.

His statement came as a shock.

"I'm flattered Wayne," I spoke to him directly. "When I said that my allegiance has moved from your mother to you, I wasn't expecting payment."

Wayne looked visibly relieved but there was an awkward silence between us.

"That said, I'd appreciate the whole story," I continued. "What's all this really about, Wayne, it's not just the money, as I believe that has been a smokescreen for my benefit all along.

"I'm ready to tell you what happened the night my father died," he said in a tone of confession.

I looked at Wayne steadily and sat back to hear the whole tragic story behind the so-called 'stolen' money.

PART FIVE – BODY IN THE TUB

CHAPTER FORTY

"Hello luv, have you had a tough day?" Diana said lovingly as she plugged the radio in and placed it on the shelf. *"I'll run you a nice warm bath. Here's the radio as there's some lovely music on tonight. You can relax and listen to Sinatra and all that."*

"Oh my," he said quite surprised at her gentle and caring thoughtfulness. *"Are you sure it's no trouble?"*

"For you, anything, my luv." She smiled as she sprinkled some bath bubbles she had managed to get on the black market, into the water.

"There you go, all ready for you."

Harry got out of his clothes and got into the lovely, steaming, bubbles and totally relaxed in the warm water to the sound of Bing Crosby's

dulcet tones.   He even joined in with a bad
rendition of "White Christmas."

*****

Wayne walked over to the large window
that overlooked the Vegas 'Strip' and began
talking as though there was no-one else in the
room, or even listening.   His trance-like state
went straight into the story.

*****

"I was walking home from the pictures
when an ambulance and police car sped past me
with blue flashing lights and bells ringing.   The
small convoy stopped just outside my house.

I picked up my pace and started running
towards home as I had an ominous feeling that
something was happening.   There were
policemen downstairs and I was stopped at the
door."

"I remember begging them to let me in and asking why the house was in darkness. They allowed me through."

"A fuse has blown and we had to switch off the main fuse board," the policeman informed me.

"I thought Geraldine would normally have come to greet me at the door but there was no sign of her. It was a Monday and this was not her usual day off that was all wrong too. The next minute I heard, *Wayne, Wayne, your father, your father*. It was Ma's desperate cries coming from the top of the stairs. Looking up I could barely make her out through the gloom but could see that she was quite hysterical, sobbing loudly with her whole body shaking. I started up the stairs and made out another shadow, in the gloom. It was a man by her side with his arm round her shoulders. I immediately recognised him as Inspector Fuller, the same police officer who had raided my father's club and arrested him. He was also the officer who arrested me for being caught in uniform. It had to be more than a coincidence. As I got nearer I could see the streaks of mascara down Ma's painted and powdered face, from the tears that were pouring from her eyes. Somehow, despite the horror of the situation I managed to find it curious that I had never seen her cry. Certainly not like this. The tears made rivulets of black run down her face, making her look almost clown-like only she wasn't smiling. Her body still shook and was wracked with an emotion I found unsettling. It would only be some years later, when I looked back on it all, that I realised what a great actress she could have been. It was an Oscar winning performance in itself!"

I stayed quiet while Wayne continued.

"I looked away from Ma and glanced into the bathroom. In that fleeting moment, I could see my Dad, floating like an old abandoned quilt. His mouth was open wide in a silent scream, his eyes bulging fiercely but it was the sight of his hands that clutched against the side of the bath that made me turn away."

Wayne paused it seemed to catch his breath.

"And then I saw it. The old Bakelite valve radio, plugged in, floating in the bathtub all twisted and melted, like a ship of doom on an eerily calm sea."

"None of it added up. For one thing, Dad never took the radio into the bathroom. I turned to Ma who was still being held close by that Inspector Fuller and asked her what happened."

"I don't really know," she sobbed. "One minute he was singing at the top of his voice to "I've Got a Gal in Kalamazoo" and the next moment, there was a piercing scream. I ran up the stairs as fast as I could and.. well."

"She paused in what appeared to be a calculated way."

"It was horrible," she added after a while.

"Your father was thrashing about in the water, he was being electrocuted by the radio that had somehow fallen into the bath. Oh God it was just too horrible to describe. "

"At this point, I noticed Fuller gripped my mother's hand and then she continued."

"My instinct told me not to touch him or I'd be electrocuted too," she said. "So I dialled 999 and waited for the Police to arrive."

"An ambulance driver came up to me and spoke quietly and considerately asking, almost apologetically, if they could remove my father from the bath.

I looked to what had become my father's ice cold watery grave. Despite my revulsion, I couldn't tear myself away from staring, as the ambulance guys lifted my Dad's wet and stiff-like body, with as much dignity as was possible. All the while, like something from a Hammer House of Horror movie, my Dad's rigid right arm seemed to point accusingly straight ahead, while the other hand gripped tightly to the edge of the porcelain bath. It seemed as if, even beyond death, he was pointing with accusation at Ma. The stench of burnt flesh was in the air – I found it choking me and suddenly had an overwhelming need to throw up. The whole grizzly scenario suddenly became too much for me to bear.

Eventually, the performance at an end, the ambulance crew and police left.

My father was certainly no angel but he didn't deserve to die like that."

****

Wayne took a deep breath and moved away from the window. He looked straight at me saying that it didn't end there.

"The lights came back on, and Inspector Fuller was the last to leave," he said. "And then a miraculous transformation came over my mother. The tears stopped almost instantly, a quick dab of the eyes and some powder to erase the lines left by them."

Wayne looked directly at me. "I think I told you the rest," he said. "She went straight to my father's bureau and got the life insurance papers but was slightly taken off balance when she knew I had seen her. My father's policy easily paid for a new bathroom and some left over. It was the left over that is at the root of her pursuit of me."

"I knew Ma was up to something, when I asked her where Geraldine was, as it wasn't her day off. She told me to mind my own business and said that all Geraldine needs to know is that my Dad had died of a heart attack. She said that Geraldine didn't need to know the sordid details."

"What about the radio?" I asked Wayne. "You said he never took the radio into the bathroom."

"I asked Ma how the radio ended up in the bathroom but she made up some cock and bull excuse saying: "*Oh you know your father, he said there was some good music on and he wanted to listen to the radio and relax in the bath, so who was I to argue with him?*""

Wayne's mimicry of her was chillingly authentic.

"She totally avoided my gaze," Wayne remembered. "She just said he probably reached out for something and snagged the wire which must have 'accidentally' knocked the radio into the bath. It was such a blatant and outrageous lie. I stood there in total disbelief. I couldn't even catch my breath."

"When Geraldine turned up for work the next day, I told her in confidence what *really* happened," Wayne said. "It was too horrible. I just felt Geraldine should know. She was truly shocked when she heard the news but kept it to herself."

I now realised why Geraldine had seemed so apprehensive and terrified when I met her at King's Cross.

Wayne continued. "Ma told her to clean out the bathroom as her first job before doing the rest of the house. She must have felt sick knowing that Dad had died in it. I suspect this was the final straw for Geraldine and although it took a while, I'm glad she eventually made the decision to leave."

"What about this Inspector Fuller?" I asked recalling what I already heard from Rob in England.

"I told you that Fuller came round the next day to check if my mother was alright," Wayne continued. "He assured her that the coroner had signed off the death certificate as heart attack to spare her feelings."

"How very convenient," I interrupted.

"Wayne I have to tell you that I have since received confirmation that the Coroner was in cohorts with Inspector Fuller and I will follow this up on my return."

Wayne nodded with a visible look of relief on his face and finally seemed to realise that I had been on his side all along.

"There is certain proof that your Ma was having an affair with Inspector Fuller and by all accounts will have been involved in your father's death," I continued. "For a start it is suspicious that he was even there in plain clothes in the house before the uniformed police arrived, which is almost unheard of in a case of this nature."

"That didn't cross my mind at the time," Wayne admitted.

"It's all starting to add up, as it bothered me at the time when I noticed him hanging about at the funeral too, away from the main congregation."

"Where the question of the money comes into the scenario is after I left for the Navy and moved on to America. I asked my mother for some money and in a way I did blackmail her. I knew she had received enough money from the life insurance to not only redecorate the bathroom but left a tidy sum for her to spend. I told her it was the least she could do to share some of the money with me, or I just might tell someone how my father really died. She never denied it and gave me a cheque for £10,000 to keep me quiet."

"Is that the whole story?" I asked.

"It's true she gave me some money but as far as I'm concerned it wasn't a loan," he responded despondently. "It was to keep me quiet and to keep her out of jail for murder. I thought it was a small price to pay."

"I've said it before and I'll say it again, I have nothing to hide. I just hope you understand, Charlie, how I feel about my mother trying to track me down.   I don't want anything more to do with her. She ruined my life and she murdered my father. End of story."

With that, we finished our drinks, he shook my hand and left the room.

CHAPTER FORTY-ONE

This was no movie.

There was no script.

There was no rehearsal.

It was, however, the final curtain.

*****

The three of us drove back from Las Vegas. It was a strange time for us, hearing Wayne tell us stories he had suppressed for such a long time. We were all fairly quiet on the drive back to Los Angeles. Although Rita was not party to the conversation I'd had with Wayne, I think he may well have told her the truth some years ago.

Only I was hearing it for the first time.

Wayne dropped us off at our various places. I was no longer in the employ of Diana Saunders and Rita and I arranged to meet

Wayne at 8pm the next day, as I only had a few days left before I had to return to the UK.

CHAPTER FORTY-TWO

The next day Rita picked me up just before 8.00pm. We drove up the steep hill leading to Miller Drive and stood outside the now familiar house at the end of the road.

We were too late.

There was something horribly wrong, I could feel it in my gut, almost that same feeling Wayne must have felt when he returned home to the darkened Saunders household that fateful night.

This time the Ambulance lights flashed an American red and there were sirens instead of bells. A police car in black and white, LAPD livery, caught us up short. I looked over at the house. There standing back and lurking in the shadow of the door I saw two figures I recognised with a creeping horror and a sinking feeling.

There was Diana Saunders standing there in all her painted glory and still in that fur coat she wore the first time I met her.

The tall figure standing next to her with his arm protectively around her shoulder in that familiar way, was unmistakably Inspector Fuller.

As I looked over at Diana Saunders, our eyes met.

Hers were full of hate and a perverse form of triumph.

At that moment, the full force of what she had done, hit me.

I felt sick to my stomach.

My eyes were drawn towards the body on the gurney being taken from the house to the ambulance.

Covered over in a white sheet, it had to be Wayne. Who else could it be?

"What happened?" I asked one of the ambulance drivers.

"Poor guy broke his neck from the fall," the ambulance driver confirmed.

"Where did he fall?" I enquired already knowing the answer.

"Off the deck," the ambulance driver continued. "The wood was rotten, an accident just waiting to happen. It's good his mother and her chap were here. I think they did as much as they could."

I bet they did, I thought.

"The cops have put a hazard tape round it."

That old nagging question came to mind: 'did he fall, or was he pushed?'

Wayne's mother I now believed was quite capable of carrying out such a deed and with the help of Inspector Fuller, poor Wayne wouldn't have stood a chance.

Wayne had carried the truth about his father to his grave and this time around, his mother had silenced him for good.

I couldn't speak. The overwhelming guilt of not warning Wayne a lot earlier that I had seen his mother here, left me speechless.

It was the soft touch on my arm that broke me from my guilty trance and Rita's gentle voice.

"Come on, there's nothing we can do here," she soothed.

"Let's go."

EPILOGUE

CHAPTER FORTY-THREE

I left LA with a heavy heart and returned to London to find 4 letters in the post lying on the floor behind the letterbox. The familiar handwriting left no doubt that it was Wayne's, like messages from beyond the grave. Clearly he had written them even before the departure to Las Vegas, in the knowledge that his mother was already sniffing around via my appearance.

The first letter was addressed to me with instructions to distribute the other 3.

There was one to Lester, one to Geraldine which were sealed but the fourth one addressed to 'Ma' was left unsealed.

His letter to me read:
Charlie, by the time you get this, I will have died one way or another, by the hand of my mother, or my illness which I never mentioned to you.

I told you that I never had any real proof of what Ma did to my father but I am writing this as a witness to her words that she conveyed to me after my father's death. The fact that Fuller, a plain clothes detective was on the scene before the uniformed police and ambulance arrived, speaks volumes and is an admission of guilt in itself.

My father never took a radio in the bathroom with him. If the case is open again, it will become evident that it is almost impossible to reach the radio when lying in the bath even though the evidence was removed when the bathroom was redecorated. It had to be knocked into the bath. He was pointing towards the door, which was exactly where Ma and Fuller must have stood, watching him being electrocuted to death. How cruel and wicked of them.

*****

Geraldine had phoned and I told her there was a letter waiting for her. She took the trip to

London and when she arrived I could see the heartbreak in her eyes. There were no words. We didn't need any. Something in the silence said it all.

I forwarded Wayne's letter to his brother, Lester.

I never opened it, but I hope Wayne was able to put in writing his real feelings towards his brother. He made Lester a benefactor in his will on condition nothing went to his mother. I suspect that he described in brief the evening his father died and Lester would have realised that his brother carried that awful knowledge with him to the day he died.

I took the opportunity to read the letter which he had left for his mother unsealed:

Ma,   These will be my last words to you. I wrote about the night of my father's death and instructed the letter to be handed to the Police.

If justice has been done, by the time you receive this letter, you may well be enjoying your new home at Her Majesty's prison. No doubt this will come as a surprise – reaching out to you from beyond the grave if you have had your way.

As for the money you were after, you know it was part of Dad's life insurance, and for what you did, you had no right to claim it at all.

From the moment I was born, thirty six years ago, my earliest recollection is of a life of turmoil, insecurity and unhappiness. I recall all too vividly violent arguments, fright, bewilderment and often being shipped off to live with other relatives and sometimes friends.

When we settled in Sidmouth Road, I was going to school but was never permitted friends home; they were either too young, too stupid, or just too many reasons why I couldn't have a friend. Lester was permitted certain privileges, which one day when I reached his age, I thought I would get, but I didn't.

I was by no means the model son or child; I pilfered money from time to time and I would get into trouble. When you argued with Dad, you would come around to be my friend, crawl out of your bed into mine. From ten years of age, I planned and schemed to leave and run away.

I went to work at the age of 14 and gave you 7/6d out of the 10 shillings I earned. I finally made the break when I lied about my age to get into the Service. I couldn't wait for my legal age to be called up. I got in to the Navy but was discharged after six months for being colour blind even that was thanks to you.

The day I came out of the Service and arrived home, I realised what a huge mistake I had made. I was being treated like a child again. I couldn't go out without returning home and being bombarded with the foulest of accusations, so I ran away.

You always upset my equilibrium. I was still having to prove to you that I could be something, still be somebody because when I was a child, it was drummed into me that I never would amount to anything. I could never do anything right, unless it was to buy you something.

When I left for the Navy, I cried all the way along the High Road and to the Station. You wouldn't have known, or even cared but when I got on the local train to the Terminus, everyone there had someone to see them off; someone who cared for them. I sat in that train alone and unwanted and watched the sight around me – I've never forgotten that loneliness.

During my time in the Navy I was among men and women and for the first time I realised that I could make friends, that people liked me and that I was wanted. I almost married but in America I had the space to find who I really was – you may have known but wouldn't acknowledge it.

When the war was over, I didn't even want to return to England; I couldn't live in the house where there was no love lost between us but then I wanted to see Dad as I heard he wasn't too well. Instead I came home to attend his funeral.

After the funeral, I left for America and I don't know why but felt sorry for you and left you my address. But your constant nagging and orders, even in writing eventually got on my nerves and I stopped replying. You just couldn't get the message that I didn't want you there. I was avoiding you because you would take away my friends as you did throughout my life.

I know you even ruined Lester's marriage. Hannah confided in me about the hold you seemed to have over Lester and your negative influence over their marriage, which ultimately led to their breakup. Then you had him all to yourself.

Just about a year ago, I started with a psychoanalyst. Not knowing the degree of my mental status, I was in pretty bad shape. Now, after almost a year of analysis, I have, with much help, sorted through the detritus of my life and unravelled most of the mental block, including the burden of my father's death. You tried to condemn him, a sane man, to an institution, for your own selfish motives and when that didn't work you murdered him instead.

I didn't realise you had such evil in your heart that you would be capable of killing. I've had to live with the evil that I witnessed. I thought I had put it behind me but every now and then I'm reminded of that night. You made me a part of it and it's an event that I cannot erase from my memory. Just as my father was a victim, I became one too.

And to the present time. You didn't have to look far for me. I had to be realistic that one day you might find me.

Your guilt drove you to find me for no other reason than it was eating away at you.

I was a witness to the murder of my father and you would go to any lengths to find me.

The consolation in all this, is that the Private Investigator you hired, will have carried out MY instructions and you will now pay for the ruined lives.

If there is an afterlife and our paths should cross, it's for the best we just ignore each other. Your son, Wayne

***

There was no love in it. But a sadness in between the lines was so deep and yet there was to be justice in this tragic story after all.

Diana Saunders went to prison and by all accounts received no visitors.   I could just see her opening the letter in her cell, reading it and dashing it away into the bin immediately after.

Even if Diana could have, there was no reason for her to reply.

Neither Diana nor Wayne had time to forgive each other.

It was Wayne's letter to the police that had led to her arrest and that of Inspector Fuller who was convicted with conspiracy and placed in solitary confinement.

And the Coroner? He was arrested too. It was always on my mind why Diana Saunders and Inspector Fuller just turned up in LA without letting me know. Turns out Fuller panicked when he learned that the Coroner, who had falsified Harry Saunders' death certificate, was under investigation for making a habit of topping up his bank balance this way. Fuller knew the investigation would eventually lead to Wayne, so he had to get to Wayne before the police did.

I, of course, never got paid.

Sometimes, in this game, there are winners and losers... This time, there were no winners and no happy ending.

Acknowledgements

Special thanks to **Dr *Roger Cottrell PhD***, the author and former investigative crime reporter, for his constructive advice and collaboration on editing this book and coming up with a gritty title too. He has guided my story into an exciting mixture of fact and fiction. His recent book, *Jaded Jerusalem*.

Also thanks to the following for being of great assistance in compiling some of the factual sections.

Aitkens, Vanoye – once a dancing partner of the famous
Katherine Dunham

Bell, Den @ Bob Mizer Foundation – *Athletic Model Guild* for background information physique photographer

Canton, Jan; Hart, Gloria; Roberts, Karl – Proof reading

Dunphy, Trent and Mainardi, Bob of San Francisco owners of *Aztec Sacrifice*

Furtado, Ken - George Quaintance author and scholar.
www.georgequaintance.com
Quaintance had many connections in Hollywood and in LA society. He designed hairstyles for Jeanette McDonald, Lillian Gish, Dietrich and Constance Bennett, and he was best buddies with Hedy Lamarr. He painted women modelling gowns by Adrian and Irene, both of whom also were important costume designers for the film studios.

Hart, Tina   - Facebook:
www.facebook.com/DebbieNymanAuthor/

Massengill, Reed   - for looking back in the files

Zinski, Elena   - creative genius for producing the
front cover. www.instagram.com/elenazinskiart

REFERENCE

pp 89,102-103,139,149-150 & Operation Meridian 268-276

The original 1830 squadron report relating to HMS Illustrious is at Royal Navy - Fleet Air Arm Museum
RNAS Yeovilton, Ilchester, Somerset, BA22 8HT
Accession No. NMRN 2023/212

The following is a true excerpt from The Scribe's *personal notes*

It was interesting to watch the Corsairs on the aprons, whose wings would fold up. *The Scribe* had never seen a plane like this before.

The first flights were to be made by the new pilots on the Squadron and *The Scribe* watched for the ten planes to return to base. The loudspeaker announced the arrival of Corsairs and for the mechanics of 1830 Squadron to 'stand by' to pick up their planes. However, only nine planes had landed and a crew of six men were standing by for their plane.

"Get out, all of you!" the Commanding Officer blurted out.

"No, not you *(Scribe)*, I need you. The rest of you get out! Send a Wire to the Commanding officer, British Squadrons, Washington DC."

"While out on an acquaintance run with Corsairs this morning, one of my planes suddenly went into a spin and crash-landed into the ocean. Require replacement of pilot and plane. A full report will follow."

The Scribe filled out the necessary Naval forms pertaining to the loss of Naval aircraft and personnel. The death of a young man who had just married before he left England, brought a dark shadow over the newly-formed Squadron.

Next day a similar routine flight was scheduled and nine planes took off. Everyone anxiously waited for their return. The mechanics sat around, twisting their rags, all were looking up into the empty sky.

"Crew of 1830 Squadron, stand-by."

The Scribe counted the planes as they began to land; one, two, three, and four made bad landings and five almost hit the runway, six was fine and so was seven. The eighth plane landed but all were, once more, looking for number nine. "Get another wire off to C.O., British Squadrons, Washington. Another plane and pilot lost. Request grounding of planes until enquiry can be made. No apparent reason can be given for both yesterday's and today's loss." The C.O. pounded his desk.

The reply came and the Squadron was informed to carry on its 'forming up routine'. Pilots felt unsure and afraid, as the mystery of the two planes went into investigation.

Everything was double-checked mechanically and old Ironside, the Squadron C.O. gave everyone a pep talk. Nobody seemed that convinced.

The air of tenseness increased as on the fourth day the pilots got into their cockpits. The eight planes taxied out on the runway and took off. They formed up in two formations of four as they winged off into infinity. The wait for their return was even longer than before. Nobody could concentrate except on the sky. A long blast suddenly shattered the silence and eardrums. *The Scribe* sat paralysed in his chair, as fire engines and an ambulance tore across the apron to the end of the runway.

"A plane is in trouble, stand by for a crash!" the loudspeaker announced.

The Scribe noticed Corsairs on the horizon; he started to count – one, two, three, now fourth was coming into view. One formation was safe but whose was it, the Commanding Officer of his Second in Command? Then the other formation started to take shape; one, two and then unbelievably in front of his eyes, one of the Corsairs started to spin; it took but seconds and then went out of view. Personnel were rushing forward from everywhere towards the runway.

"Keep the Runway clear for landing aircraft," the loudspeaker announced.

There was only six planes but there should be seven.

All planes were grounded by a wire from Washington and a full investigation was eventually held.